JAWS

The bandits s[...] onto the riverbank, howling and wav[...] weapons. Some held torches in the gathering dusk. Shots rang out. Uncle Richard paddled faster. "Move it!" he shouted.

Stephen hunched over the log, and turned his eyes to the river. "There's another log," he said. "But how can it go against the current?"

The log opened its mouth, showing Stephen a row of sharp teeth. "A-a-alligator!" he yelled. His grip on the log loosened, and he fell sideways into the river.

Race Against Time

Watch out for more titles in the series!

RACE AGAINST TIME™

Search for Mad Jack's Crown

J. J. Fortune

Armada

First published in the U.S.A. in 1984 by
Dell Publishing Co., Inc., New York.
First published in the U.K. in Armada in 1985
by Fontana Paperbacks,
8 Grafton Street,
London W1X 3LA.

Race Against Time is a trademark of
Dell Publishing Co., Inc., New York.

Illustrations by Bill Sienkiewicz
Map by Giorgetta Bell McRee

Printed in Great Britain by
William Collins Sons & Co. Ltd., Glasgow

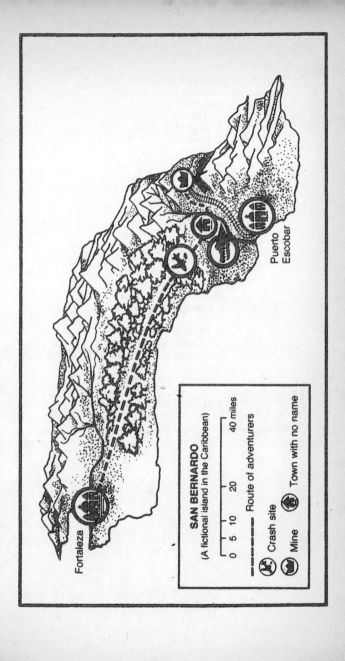

SAN BERNARDO
(A fictional island in the Caribbean)

0 5 10 20 40 miles

------ Route of adventurers

🏃 Crash site
⛏ Mine
🏘 Town with no name

Puerto Escobar

Fortaleza

CONTENTS

1

UPS AND DOWNS

SATURDAY; 7:14 A.M., *San Bernardo*

Stephen Lane had seen many plane crashes in the movies. But this time he had a front row seat—in the crashing plane.

"Watch out for that tree," he shouted to the pilot as she fought with the controls, her heart-shaped face taut. The plane pulled level again, just missing the treetop. But a fresh buffet of wind sent it lurching off to the side.

"*Viento estúpido*," the pilot grumbled as she wrestled with the wheel. Suddenly a new gust hurled the plane up into the air. Stephen was thrown back in his seat. And I was the one who wanted to sit in the co-pilot's seat for the view! he said to himself.

The pilot straightened out the little Cessna, and for a few seconds it flew like a plane instead of a roller coaster. Then the winds went back to playing catch with it. The plane dived straight down. Stephen stared in horror as the ground came rocketing up at him.

A hand came over the back of Stephen's seat and touched his shoulder. He jumped, then aimed a dirty look at the seat behind his. "Uncle Richard! What are you trying to do? Scare me to death?"

The plane pulled out of the dive. Uncle Richard shouted over the drone of the straining engine. "Oh, keep your shirt on. It's just a little breezy out there." The plane rattled in a new gust.

Stephen turned in his seat to see if his uncle was serious. "Little breezes don't try to tear your wings off," he said.

The pilot cut in. "You're the ones in a hurry. Couldn't wait for the wind to die down." Everyone was thrown to one side as the plane bounced sideways. *"Gringos locos!"* she grumbled.

Stephen lowered his voice as he leaned over to Uncle Richard. "I think she's mad at us."

"What gives you that idea?"

"She keeps muttering in Spanish."

Uncle Richard's head came forward. "What's she saying?"

"Well, she said something about *viento stúpido.*"

"Viento estúpido means stupid wind. Did she say anything else?"

"Gringos locos," Stephen said.

Uncle Richard smiled. "That means . . ."

"I know what that means," Stephen said. "She's right!"

The pilot turned to him. "I'm glad somebody agrees with me."

Stephen turned around, his mouth open. He clamped it shut. "You heard everything?"

The pilot's eyes twinkled. "You have to talk pretty loud to be heard in here, kid."

"Oh, boy. Look, I'm sorry, Miss . . . Señorita Sotelo," Stephen stammered.

She grinned, eyes on her controls. "Don't worry about it. And stop being so formal. My full name is Alicia Juana Maria de Cervera Velez y Sotelo, but everyone called me Al when I went to school in California."

Stephen was silent for a second. "Uh . . . Al?" he said. "When will we get to the mine?"

"It's only a fifteen-minute ride in good weather," Al said. The winds began shaking the plane again. "It's this up-and-down flying that's holding us back."

Stephen shifted in his seat and looked down. Everything below had changed since they had taken off from the town of Fortaleza. The terrain had been open—houses and small farms. Now it looked as if they were flying over a giant green rug. But Stephen knew that the rug was made up of treetops, thousands upon thousands of them—a whole jungle full of them.

As he watched, the jungle gave way to a big patch of open land. "There's the old Portillo farm," Uncle Richard said, pointing. "The only cleared spot in the area. In a few minutes we'll cross the Peligroso River. Then we'll be into the mountains, and landing at my mine."

Stephen looked down to see men with sticks in the clearing.

"What are those men?" he asked. "Farmers?"

The cockpit window shattered in his face. Stephen jumped back, and something zinged past his ear.

"Bandits!" Uncle Richard's voice cut across the noise. "Al, get us out of here!"

"Just what we need—*bandidos*," Al growled as her hands stabbed at the controls. The engine drone rose up to a higher pitch, and the plane shot forward.

Stephen looked down at the men. Their sticks still spat fire at the plane. Uncle Richard patted his shoulder. "Those old rifles aren't too accurate," he said.

Stephen gulped for breath as a line of holes appeared across the instrument panel. "I hope you know what you're talking about," he yelled.

"We'll be out of range in a second," Uncle Richard said. The engine began making funny noises. "Unless, of course, they nicked our fuel line . . ."

Stephen turned to Al. "Are we okay?"

Al didn't answer him—she just sat there with the controls in her hands, her eyes closed. Slowly she fell forward. The plane nosed down.

"Miss? *Señorita?* Al?" Stephen grabbed her shoulder. Al's hands fell from the controls and she rolled into Stephen's lap. A thin trickle of blood ran down the side of her head.

For a second Stephen's mouth hung open. Then, "UNCLE RICHARD!"

But Uncle Richard's powerful arms were already

over Stephen's seat, lunging for the controls. The plane began gaining altitude again.

"Get her sitting straight. She'll have to wait for a minute. And you, out of your seat. I've got to get in there."

Stephen pushed Al up in her seat, then unbuckled his seat belt. "I'm ready," he said, looking at Uncle Richard. But Uncle Richard stared intently at the front of the plane. Smoke and little tongues of flame danced around the engine. "A fire?" Stephen said. "What next?"

"No time to waste. You'll have to steer us out of this, Steve." Uncle Richard's hands whipped out over Stephen's head and began punching buttons. "When I say now! you push straight forward on the wheel."

Uncle Richard's fingers hit a few more buttons and he shouted "now!" The engine went off. Stephen pushed. The plane started to zoom straight for the ground.

"Are you trying to crash us?" Stephen yelled. He wanted to say more, but his tongue seemed to be stuck. His hands clenched the wheel. He watched his knuckles turn white.

"We're diving to blow out that fire," Uncle Richard said.

"But how will we know when to stop?" Stephen's eyes ran over the smashed dials of the instrument panel.

Uncle Richard held out his wristwatch and began flicking buttons. "I'll use the echo ranger," he said.

From the corner of his eye Stephen saw tiny lights glitter on the dial.

Stephen could have done the same thing with his watch. But that would have meant releasing his death grip on the controls. "What does it say?"

"If my calculations are right, and we have a bit of luck, we'll put the fire out well before we hit the trees." The number *50* appeared on the dial. "Fifty feet before we hit them."

The plane had been eerily silent with the engine dead. Now they heard the scream of air rushing through the shattered windows as they fell. Stephen glanced from the fire to the ground.

A green wall rushed up in front of the plane. The smoke had cleared away. "Steve! Pull back on the wheel!" Uncle Richard hit buttons. The engine coughed, sputtered, and started droning again. Then the plane began to climb.

"That was a bit close," Uncle Richard said, breathless.

"A bit close?" Stephen said.

Just then an icy blast roared through the cockpit, hitting the plane like a hammer. The controls tore out of Stephen's hands as the plane went spinning away. Again the trees came swooping up at them. This time the plane went plowing into the branches.

Stephen heard the sound of splintering wood as they tore through the treetops. The sunlight came in flashes now as they swept past branches, smashing through everything in their path. A huge bough came up before them. They rushed at it, rammed into it, and stopped.

Uncle Richard was flung forward against the back of Stephen's seat. But Stephen flew right out the broken window. His mouth opened in a silent scream as he whirled into the trees. Leaves slashed at his face. They whipped through his fingers as he grabbed desperately. Plant juices made his hands slimy as he grabbed at a branch. He caught it, but began to slip. Throwing his body at the branch, Stephen got an arm around it. He clung tightly and kicked until he managed to get a leg around the branch too. Then he lay there, breathing heavily.

Stephen shook his head hard, partly to clear his mind but mostly to get his hair out of his eyes. He should have listened when Mom told him to get a haircut.

The plane's gone, he thought, peering up into the treetops. And so is Uncle Richard. He shut his eyes. We've come through some pretty tough scrapes together, but getting us stranded in the jungle—this is the worst yet. How did I get into this? He sighed. With Uncle Richard, it was easy.

2

MINERAL INVESTMENTS

FRIDAY; 6:36 P.M., *New York*

Only the day before, Stephen had come dashing down the stairs of his family's brownstone in New York City, skidding to a halt when he heard voices in Dad's den. Dad was talking with Uncle Richard. ". . . so we get a great investment credit, and still keep liquid . . ." It was clear that Dad was talking business. And Stephen knew better than to interrupt him.

"It's a pretty sweet deal," Dad went on. Uncle Richard smiled and nodded. "You've got to protect yourself, Richard. They'll cut your throat out there, you know." Dad drew his finger along his neck. "Don't be afraid to ask for help. I'd be happy to go over your portfolio . . ."

Stephen grinned. It was Dad's once-a-month attempt to find out where Uncle Richard got all his money. As far as Dad knew, Richard Duffy had spent a dozen years as a globe-trotting engineer when he moved into the top floor apartment. He had no furniture, hardly any luggage, but lots of cash. Dad was still curious.

It wasn't surprising. Dad was the James T. Lane of James T. Lane and Associates, Investment Counselors. He liked to know about money. But Uncle Richard had nothing to say about it.

"I'm always grateful to you, Jim," Uncle Richard said. "Without you and Marion I wouldn't have a real home. But money isn't a problem for me."

"I hope it always stays that way," Dad said. "I still don't see how you could retire at thirty-four on savings from your salary. I'm only eight years older than you are, and I'm still working like a maniac."

Uncle Richard grinned. "I always got top pay, but there was no place to spend it. My money is safe enough. You might say it's heavily involved in minerals."

"Minerals, eh?" Dad began as Mom swept into the room, interrupting him.

"You shouldn't listen at doorways, Stephen. All packed, Jim?" Mom stood there, looking very trim in her new navy blue business suit, holding a pair of plane tickets in her hand.

"Yes, indeed!" Dad laughed. "Chicago, here we come! What do you think a health-food convention will be like, Richard?"

"Healthy?" Uncle Richard said.

"It will be businesslike," Mom said, giving Dad and Uncle Richard her evil eye. "And Oh, Nuts! is my business, just like your firm is yours, dear."

"You make a bigger deal about that health-food store of yours than you do about my firm."

Mom smiled sweetly. "In five years it *will* be bigger than your firm."

"*I* think you'll both have a lot of fun in Chicago," Uncle Richard said quickly.

"I hope so." Mom looked troubled. "And I hope everything will be okay back here."

"You'd think this was the first time I ever stayed with Stephen," Uncle Richard said.

"Every time you're alone with him I worry." Mom looked hard at Uncle Richard.

He smiled at her a little nervously. "Aren't you making a big deal about nothing? It's just for the weekend, after all. We'll spend it sitting around the house."

That was true for fifteen minutes.

Then the doorbell rang and Stephen thought it was his parents coming back for something they'd forgotten. But when Uncle Richard pulled open the door, a big, burly man in a rumpled suit was standing there. He had a squashed nose and the biggest, hairiest ears that Stephen had ever seen.

"Cutthroat, you old pirate!" Uncle Richard stepped to the doorway and grabbed the man's hand. Then he stopped. "Uh, Steve, this is my old friend, Mr. Morton. This is my nephew, Stephen."

Mr. Morton took Stephen's hand and smiled. It

was a scary sort of smile: the lips moved, but the eyes didn't join in. They would have looked the same if he'd frowned, except the frown might have been scarier. "Nobody's called me mister in more years than I can remember, Duffy," he said. "Which don't matter to me. I got some information you might like to know. About that gold mine of yours."

"Gold mine?" Stephen whirled to look at Uncle Richard. "You get your money from a *gold mine?*"

Cutthroat looked from Stephen to Uncle Richard and began to laugh, *har-har-har*. "Duffy, you are some piece of work! Man! If I had a gold mine, I'd be telling the whole world about it!"

He looked at Stephen. "Your uncle did a job for this guy, and the guy pays him off with this gold mine down in San Bernardo. The guy thinks it's a bum mine, see—it got gold in it, but there's no way to make it pay. But since your uncle is a good engineer, besides other things . . ."

Stephen nodded. He was sure there were lots of "other things" Uncle Richard had been up to.

". . . he came up with machinery to make the mine profitable."

"I get a check at the end of every month," Uncle Richard said. "Enough to *let me retire*." He looked hard into Cutthroat's eyes as he said that.

"You're gonna get a surprise this month," Cutthroat said. "They ain't digging gold there anymore."

Stephen watched Uncle Richard change from easy-going uncle to dangerous man. It always scared him a little. Uncle Richard's eyes went steely gray. He stepped back from the doorway, tensed for a fight. "I suppose you have proof?"

Cutthroat Morton stepped into the house. "Right here," he said, pointing behind himself. From behind his bulk another man stepped out. He hardly came up to Cutthroat's belt buckle, and he was dressed in a rumpled suit too.

He held a letter. As he reached to put it into Uncle Richard's hand, his coat gaped open, and Stephen saw something he'd seen only in movies—a pistol in a shoulder holster.

"So, Wally, still hanging around with old Cutthroat," Uncle Richard said. Wally just smiled as Uncle Richard took the letter and began to read.

"Recognize who the writer is?" Cutthroat asked.

"It's Pablo, one of the foremen at my mine," Uncle Richard said. "He's asking to come live with his brother since he and all the mine workers have been fired." He looked up.

"But I didn't fire anyone. Where did you get this?" His lips twisted. "Maybe that's an awkward question."

Cutthroat looked at his shoes. "Let's just say a mail train got robbed, and this wound up in my hands," he said, stepping back to the door. "Take it easy."

"Hold it." Uncle Richard pulled out his wallet. "You only come up to New York when you need to bankroll an operation." He counted out ten crisp one-hundred-dollar bills. "That should at least get you started."

Cutthroat looked at the money. "We ain't always seen eye to eye, Duffy," he said. "But I gotta admit, you got class."

Wally's gold tooth flashed as he grinned. Cutthroat opened the door.

"Where are you going?" Stephen asked.

Cutthroat's face turned black. It wasn't smiling. "Kid, that ain't a smart question."

Uncle Richard nudged Stephen. "Cutthroat is a bit touchy about telling people where he's going. He's afraid the police might be waiting." He shook hands with Cutthroat and Wally. "Take care."

Closing the door, Uncle Richard said, "Bad news. I've got to get down to San Bernardo right away."

He looked at Stephen. "Now, what are we going to do about you?"

Stephen burst out, "You're as bad as Mom sometimes!"

Uncle Richard looked guilty. "Don't remind me! She worries about you, and she doesn't trust me. If she only knew how right she was!"

Stephen knew why his uncle was worried. They had faced a lot of danger together—from their first adventure, *Revenge in the Silent Tomb*, to their most recent escapade, *Pursuit of the Deadly Diamonds*.

"So what are you going to do, put me in a day-care center while you're away?"

"Wouldn't think of it. How could I endanger all those children by leaving you with them?" Uncle Richard sighed. "I keep my endangering in the family. Okay. Come along."

"I'll go and pack."

"No time. Just get your watch." He looked at his own wrist and began hitting the buttons. "Meanwhile, I have some figuring to do. We've got to get there and back before your folks come home," he said. "They're due at ten P.M. on Sunday. That gives us . . ." Numbers marched across the dial as Uncle Richard tapped tiny buttons on the watch. Stephen was always fascinated to watch him work it. Uncle Richard's Kronom K-D2 was the only thing in the world he wouldn't part with. Part computer, part watch, he could make it do everything except sit up and bark. Stephen had one hidden in his room—a gift from Uncle Richard—but he still gazed in fascination as numbers flew like sparks on the dial.

"Fifty four," Uncle Richard finally said.

"Fifty-four what?"

"Fifty-four hours before your folks get back. I've got the San Bernardo flights programmed into this . . ."

More flicking, more lights. "We've got to leave right now. That'll get us down there by 11:30 tonight. You can sleep in the hotel. I'll get supplies and a plane . . . be ready to leave by dawn. Get to the mine by seven in the morning . . . give me a day to straighten things out . . ." He slapped his hand on the desk. "Perfect! Let's move it!"

A voice broke into Stephen's thoughts. "Steve? That you down there?"

Stephen looked up to see Uncle Richard framed by a hole in the greenery. "Wondered where you flew off to," he said. "Well, you look all right. Let's get you over to this tree."

"What do you mean?"

"The branch you're holding on to is on one tree. The branch I'm standing on belongs to another. My tree has the plane stuck on it, so it would be a good idea if you came over here."

"Fine," Stephen said. "But how do I get there?"

"Look down. See that branch about ten feet below you?"

Stephen moved on his perch. It began to sway alarmingly, but he saw the branch Uncle Richard meant. "I see it."

"It's connected to this tree. All you have to do is drop down to it. Then you can crawl along until you get up here to me."

"Wait a second," Stephen said. "You expect me to drop down to that branch? How do you know I'll catch it?"

"You can do it—you're tall for your age. Anyway, you caught the one you're on, didn't you?"

"Just barely. And I'm not jumping down there."

"Would it change your mind if I told you there was a big snake coming out on your branch?"

Stephen looked up at Uncle Richard. "This is no time to be kidding," he said. Then he heard a slithering sound. He looked into the shadows and saw something moving—a diamond-shaped head and a speckled body that must have been twelve feet long.

"Wh-what is it?" Stephen asked.

"A boa constrictor. If it gets you, it will squeeze you to death. Move, Steve. Now!"

Suddenly Stephen felt something curl around his wrist. The snake had caught him!

There's only one way out of this, Stephen thought. He let the branch go and fell through the air, aiming for the branch Uncle Richard had pointed out. But he never made it. His feet inches above the branch, he jerked to a stop. The relentless pressure on his wrist told him that the snake, coiled around the branch above, still had him in its grip. Gritting his teeth against the pain, Stephen dangled helplessly.

3

PURSUED BY BANDITS

SATURDAY; 7:48 A.M., *San Bernardo*

"Grab that branch in front of you!" Uncle Richard
yelled. Stephen grabbed the branch and pulled himself closer to it.

"Bash the snake's head against it!"

Holding tight with one arm, Stephen swung his
trapped wrist down hard against the branch—once,
twice, three times. The snake's hold loosened for an
instant, then tightened. Stephen could scarcely feel
his hand anymore. Desperately he smacked his wrist
again and again. A twig on the branch splintered,
leaving a sharp stump. Stephen took a deep breath and
jammed the boa against the stump with all his might.

The snake lost its stranglehold. Stephen hauled
his arm free just as the boa began to fall. "Lost its
grip," he muttered, climbing up to Uncle Richard.

"Are you all right?" he asked, taking Stephen's wrist in his hands. Stephen winced as Uncle Richard's fingers probed. "Nothing broken. You may get a nice bruise there."

"Where's the plane?" Stephen asked.

Uncle Richard pointed up. Stephen followed his arm and saw a wing tip. "We've got a bit of a climb to get to it," his uncle said.

When they reached the plane Stephen was amazed. "It's not messed up at all," he said. Indeed, it looked as if the plane had come down for a perfect landing—but on top of a tree.

Uncle Richard climbed onto the wing and walked up to the cockpit. Al was still slumped in her seat. Uncle Richard checked the bandage wound about her long dark hair.

"Is she all right?" Stephen asked.

"She's fine. A bullet grazed her. There isn't even any bleeding now." Stephen sat down on the wing. "Softest crash I ever saw," Uncle Richard said. "We really were lucky."

"Does that mean the plane is okay?"

Uncle Richard shook his head. "Not really. There's no way we can fly out of this tree. Terrible. Wrecks our schedule." He started pulling supplies out onto the wing. "We've got a long walk ahead of us. But first, let's get these supplies down from the tree. Then we'll take Al down."

A groggy voice said, "Al will take *herself* down." They turned to see Al blinking up at them.

"Fine," Uncle Richard said. "Just remember, we're

around if you need us.'' He looked at his watch. "Let's get going."

"What's the hurry?'' Al asked.

"Those people who shot at us. We didn't fly too far before we crashed. They'll be coming along to check things out.''

That was a good enough reason for Al. Stephen was amazed at how fast they got down to solid ground. Uncle Richard handed out canteens and some cans of food. He wore a machete on one hip, a pistol on the other. Al wore a pistol too.

"What about this?'' Uncle Richard hefted a rifle. "It was on the plane.''

"Oh, keep it,'' Al said. "It's probably the last useful thing left on my poor plane.'' She looked up at the wreck. "I hope you realize this is going to be on your bill.''

Uncle Richard slung the rifle over his shoulder. "We'll worry about that later. Right now, we'd better move it.'' His machete sliced through the underbrush.

Dim sunlight glimmered on the ground under the trees. The branches filtered most of the light out. Everything was warm and clammy. Beneath their feet leaves and unidentifiable things had decayed into a mush. Al wobbled on her feet as she marched along. Sweat dripped into Stephen's eyes, burning them. He blinked.

Uncle Richard found an animal trail, and the walking got a little easier. He put Al in the lead and hung back, listening. Finally he sent Al and Stephen ahead while he moved back along the trail. Minutes later he caught up with them. "Into the brush," he said.

They pushed into the thicket at the side of the trail. Uncle Richard checked his guns. "There are six men riding mules. They're trailing us, all right."

Al pulled out her own gun. "How soon before they get here?"

"Soon enough. I could hear them joking, making no effort to keep quiet. They don't think we'll be much trouble."

Al snapped a fresh clip of bullets into her pistol. She and Uncle Richard looked at each other and smiled. "Let's change their minds," she said.

Stephen tried not to let his excitement show while they talked. Now Uncle Richard turned to him. "I want you farther down the trail."

"You mean I won't see the fight?"

"That's exactly what I mean," Uncle Richard said. "Get back into the bush, and keep low. Don't put your head up until one of us comes to get you."

"But . . ."

"Your uncle is right," Al said. "This will go better if we don't have to worry about you."

Stephen thought about that for a second. "Uncle Richard, are you sure this is all going to turn out okay?"

He smiled. "I've been in spots like this since before you were born." He pointed down the trail. "Get going."

Stephen went about twenty feet down the trail. He crawled into the bushes as Al and Uncle Richard took

up hiding places. Stephen waited for something to
happen. He didn't have to wait long.

Voices came down the trail, and the jingling of
reins. Then the bandits came into sight. Stephen
didn't know what he was expecting—big sombreros,
ammunition belts maybe. Most of the men wore old
army fatigues. They would have looked at home in
any subway station back in New York, except for the
mules and the rifles.

One of the six wore a spotless white suit and
talked in a loud voice. Aha! The boss, Stephen thought.
But if he was the boss, he wasn't too good at it. He
yelled at the men, trying to make them hurry up. His
band paid no attention to him. They rode behind one
man, who kept looking at the trail.

The tracker suddenly pulled back on his reins and
turned around. A gun went off and sent his hat
spinning.

The bandits hauled up and began blazing away at
the underbrush with their rifles. Bullets shredded the
bushes. Stephen watched the branches over his head
get torn to bits as the bullets kept going. He pushed
himself deeper into the muck. Keep your head down—
good advice.

One bandit fell off his mule. It ran down the trail
at full speed, hooves pounding right in front of
Stephen's eyes.

The bandits picked up their wounded friend. Their
shouting got uglier as they circled around, trying to
see where the shooting came from. Their mules brayed
in panic.

Then Al popped out of the bushes, her pistol in hand.

One of the riders saw her and raised his rifle for a shot. But Uncle Richard appeared and blew the gun out of his hands. The man bawled in terror, pulled his mule around, and ran for it. That was all the others needed. They turned and followed him, plowing past the leader. Bellowing, he viciously spurred his mule, charging straight at Uncle Richard.

4

THE SAGA OF MAD JACK JENSON

Uncle Richard had no time to move—the mule was almost on top of him. He pointed his gun into the air and fired it. The mule reared back from the flash and noise, flipping the rider out of the saddle. He landed flat on his back in the muck, and lay with a silly expression on his face as his mule thundered off down the trail.

Uncle Richard's gun was still in his hand as he stood over the man. "Well, Antonio, I didn't expect to see another snake so soon."

Stephen crawled out of the underbrush and walked down the path. Uncle Richard gestured with his pistol, saying, "Meet Antonio Malvado. He is—or was— the manager of my mine."

The man on the ground looked up and said, "Señor

Duffy, how glad I am to see you! You have saved me from those bandits!'' He sat up.

"Stay on the ground, Antonio. From where I was standing, it looked like you were leading those bandits.''

Antonio's hand rested on his boot top. Suddenly he whipped a knife out of a hidden sheath. "And what if I was?'' he snarled, stabbing up at Uncle Richard's stomach.

Uncle Richard twisted. The knife barely grazed his shirt. Antonio tried to recover from his lunge, but Uncle Richard was on him. He grabbed Antonio's knife hand and brought the wrist down hard on his knee. The knife went flying. Uncle Richard sent Antonio flying in the opposite direction.

Then Uncle Richard picked the knife up and went on as if nothing had happened. "Okay. Tell me why you fired my men and joined this bunch of crooks.''

Antonio's eyes glittered. "The treasure,'' he said. "Jenson's crown.''

"Whose what?'' Stephen asked.

Al answered. "Mad Jack Jenson—the pirate. He lived about three hundred years ago. Called himself the King of the Caribbean, even made himself a crown from jewels he'd stolen. The gold came from a secret mine that was supposed to be here in San Bernardo—''

Uncle Richard interrupted. "So what happened to this Jenson character?''

"A Spanish royal fleet attacked the pirate den at Fortaleza,'' she said. "It sank all the ships, and all the pirates who were captured were hanged. But some ran off into the mountains, and no one knows what happened to Mad Jack and his crown.''

"I bet you have some idea,'' Uncle Richard said, poking Antonio with his pistol.

Antonio flinched away from the gun. ''Those men behind us, they're descendants of Mad Jack's pirates. They have a letter that tells what happened to Jenson.''

Uncle Richard turned to Al. ''Is all this possible?''

She shrugged. ''There are many descendants of the buccaneers in San Bernardo. That's why so many of us speak English. And a few of them still play pirate— only they steal on land rather than on the sea.'' She prodded Antonio with her foot. ''Tell us about this letter.''

"It was written by René Le Vac, one of Mad Jack's captains. Somehow it came into the hands of Paul Le Vac, who leads the mountain bandits now. The letter curses Mad Jack for betraying his men. Jenson made his gold mine into a stronghold—just in case. When they lost at Fortaleza, Jenson, Le Vac, and a few others ran for the mine. It was full of traps that could be set once they were safely inside.

"Jenson went in first, waving his crown and raving that no one would take it away from him. When his men went to follow him, they found he had turned on the traps.''

Uncle Richard turned away. ''Traps! Crowns! Pirates!'' he snorted. ''What has this fairy tale got to do with my mine?''

"Your mine and Mad Jack's—they are the same!''

Antonio said. "The workers dug a new shaft, as you know. They struck old tunnels, very old, more than two hundred years old."

"So you told Le Vac about it and got rid of Pablo and the others." Uncle Richard looked as if he'd just seen something moving on his dinner plate. "And you decided to get rid of me when I came to check things out." He stopped for a second, and his gun came up again. "But how did you know I was here?"

Antonio smiled at Al. "We have our ways, don't we, *señorita*?"

"Fortaleza is crawling with people who'd sell information for pennies," she said, shrugging.

Uncle Richard poked Antonio again. "You'll give me information for free. What's happened at the mine?"

"Nothing. Le Vac sent scouts into the old workings, but none have returned. It seems the traps are still operating."

"How nice," Uncle Richard said. "Next question. Where is the main group of bandits?"

Antonio pressed his lips together.

"I'll make him talk," Al said, raising her pistol to Antonio's head.

"He's trying to slow us down." Uncle Richard peered back along the trail. "We'll find them when we bump into them."

Antonio grabbed Uncle Richard's trouser leg. "They are all between you and Fortaleza. You have no chance of getting back through the jungle alive. You have only one hope." He smiled. "Surrender. Trust me. I will talk with Le Vac."

"I wouldn't trust you as far as I could throw you," Uncle Richard said, yanking Antonio to his feet. "Let's get moving."

"You will die if you go down that trail," Antonio insisted. "The bandits will be waiting for you."

Uncle Richard smiled. "That's why we'll go *up* the trail. Let's see if we can't beat them to that treasure. Move it."

The rest of the day Stephen spent marching. Whenever he thought an hour or so had passed, his watch told him it was only five minutes. Finally he stopped looking. He was sweat-stained and staggering by the time Uncle Richard called a rest stop. "This trail leads to a ferrying point—a few houses and a ferryboat," he said. A brief smile flitted across Antonio's face. "Can we have something to eat?" Stephen asked.

"Here you go," Al said. She cut the top off a can with her knife. Stephen looked inside to see a pink mass.

"What is it?"

"It's corned beef hash," Uncle Richard said, opening a can for himself. "That's all that was on the plane."

Stephen took the can and dug into the hash with a spoon. "If this were an everyday Saturday," he said, "I'd just have gotten up to watch TV when we were shot down. And right now we'd be having supper."

He chewed the hash and swallowed. "I never thought I'd miss Mom's nut cutlets and puréed squash."

Uncle Richard laughed as he knelt by Stephen, chewing on some hash. He spread a map across his knee and worked with his watch. "Ten minutes from the mine by plane. But a whole day to walk fifteen miles. We'll be lucky to get across the river by nightfall."

"So what?" Stephen sat with a big glob of hash on his spoon. "We don't have a plane, and we're walking away from the airport. Whatever happens, we'll never get home on time."

Uncle Richard pushed buttons on his watch. "Not true. If we get to the mine early tomorrow, I can handle things there and still get us home ahead of your parents."

Stephen felt a glimmer of hope until he remembered all those bandits lurking somewhere out there. *If* we get home, he thought, scraping out the last of the hash.

Uncle Richard gathered the cans and threw them into the brush. Then it was back to the trail. Maybe it was the food, maybe they were getting used to the marching, or maybe it was the thought of the bandits on the trail, but they made much better time than they had before.

Antonio was the one that held them up. "These are riding boots. They aren't made for a walk through the jungle," he said, rubbing his feet.

"Maybe you'd like to walk without the boots," Al suggested.

"Can I help it if my feet hurt?" Antonio said.

"I'll take your mind off your feet!" Al flared, her hand going to her holster.

"You shouldn't let him get you going like that," Uncle Richard said. He turned to Antonio. "He's just doing what every good prisoner would do. Slow us up so his friends can come along and rescue him. Right, Antonio?"

Antonio just gave him a tight-lipped smile.

"You think that pig Le Vac is going to come and rescue you?" Al laughed bitterly. "*Zonzo!* Fool!"

"She may have a point," Uncle Richard said quietly. "Are you sure you're so valuable to Le Vac that he'd go to the trouble of rescuing you?"

The smile on Antonio's face wavered. He still didn't say a word. But he also didn't complain anymore. And his feet seemed to get better miraculously.

They marched along in silence for a while, listening to the jungle noises. Finally Stephen said, "Is it my imagination, or is it getting even damper than usual around here?"

"You're right," Uncle Richard said. "We must be close to the river now."

"*Buenos días,*" another voice said.

They turned around to see a little old man smiling at them—with a shotgun in his hands.

5

THE TOWN WITH NO NAME

SATURDAY; 6:39 P.M., *San Bernardo*

For a long moment they stood looking at the man.
Stephen noticed two things about him: The man had
no teeth, and his gun was covered with rust. Uncle
Richard noticed it too. *"Buenos días,"* he said. "Better
watch out with that thing. It might blow up on you."

The man smiled. *"Gringos?"* he said. "You sure
pick a strange place to go. Dangerous jungle out
there. You come with me to town. I guard it." He
rattled the old shotgun.

Uncle Richard looked doubtful for a second. "You
get food too," the man said.

"That does it," said Stephen. "Where do we go?"

"You know, he's got a point," said Al.

Uncle Richard laughed. "Okay, as long as it isn't
corned beef hash."

The man led them along the trail, which widened eventually into a clearing. A handful of houses stood along the trail between the jungle and a wide, muddy river, the Peligroso, Stephen guessed. The houses were simply cane walls topped with straw. "One good wind and this whole place would blow away," Al muttered.

Uncle Richard paid no attention to her. "What is this place called?" he asked the old man.

"Town got no name," he replied.

"Figures," said Al. Work in the town stopped as the few inhabitants stood and gawked at the newcomers. The old man marched along as if he were leading a parade. "Well, at least we made the old guy's day," Al whispered to Stephen.

The man led them to the water's edge and the sturdiest building they had seen yet. It was a massive log cabin topped with thatch. An addition was being built onto it. Piles of big logs were piled around outside. And just beyond, in the water, was the ferry, a brightly painted boat, bobbing empty in the river.

Uncle Richard took it all in. "The local fortress," he said quietly, nodding at the shutters with loopholes cut in them for guns. The old man followed his eyes. "For the *bandidos*," he said, shaking his ancient shotgun. He glanced at Antonio. "They are bad men."

A woman stood in the open door of the cabin. Stephen blinked. "She looks just like a gypsy; I didn't think people really wore those costumes outside of the movies," he whispered to Al. The costume showed off the woman's proud figure, and matched her stormy eyes and wild, dark hair.

"I am Maria," she said. "Would you like a drink?"

"Actually we would like some food," Al cut in before Uncle Richard could say anything.

"Oh, yes. You must be hungry," Maria said. "Come into the *cantina*."

They followed her inside and found benches and tables filling most of the room.

"I saw the ferryboat outside," Uncle Richard said to Maria. "We'd like to cross the river."

"You have half an hour to wait," Maria said. "A man is coming with some chickens, and the crew waits for him." She smiled. "We have *garbanzos* and rice ready now, and I will prepare something special for you."

Everyone except Stephen sat down with bottles of warm beer—he got a bottle of warm soda. "Not safe to drink the water around here," Al said, looking toward the kitchen. "I hope that something special doesn't turn out to be lizard gizzards."

Stephen didn't care. The rice and chick-peas tasted good, a lot better than corned beef hash, and it was a relief to sit down, even if it was on a splintery bench. He shoveled the food in and washed it down with the soda.

"Our second course seems to be taking a while," Uncle Richard said, glancing at the kitchen.

Antonio sniffed the air. "Can't tell what it is," he said. "But it smells funny."

"I think it's burning," Al said.

Suddenly the two watches began piping out warning beeps. Stephen stared at his wrist. ''Smoke detector!'' Uncle Richard shouted. ''Too much smoke for a simple meal!''

Stephen jumped to his feet. But a good lungful of the strange smoke made him giddy. He shook his head. ''What is this stuff?''

''Vegetable alkaloids, burned and carried in the smoke,'' Uncle Richard said.

''In other words, poison gas.'' Stephen looked around. The room was filling rapidly with the smoke. ''We've got to get out of here!''

That was when the heavy cabin door slammed shut. Antonio began pounding on it. ''They're bracing it from the other side!'' he gasped.

Al had already raced to the windows, but they were jammed shut too. ''No air coming from those little slots,'' she said, shaking her head woozily in the smoke.

Stephen rushed to the kitchen door, hoping to put out the fire. The room was incredibly hot, and he saw why. An old-fashioned stove was stuffed with weeds. They smoldered and threw off a wall of smoke.

He crawled along the floor to take advantage of what little fresh air was in the room. But the smoke got heavier as he got closer to the source. Trying to hold his breath, Stephen edged closer to the stove. He stretched out his hand to grab some of the weeds. As if in self-defense, a tongue of flame licked out toward him. Stephen pulled his hand back, gasping. The gasp turned into a cough, the cough into a deep breath, and suddenly the room was whirling around him. . . .

6

DANGEROUS REPTILES

SATURDAY; 7:03 P.M., *San Bernardo*

Stephen's arms and legs felt like lead. He was coughing violently, too weak to move. Yet he found himself moving. It took him a moment to realize a hand had clamped around his left ankle and dragged him to safety. Well, not exactly safety. The room outside was almost as full of deadly smoke as the kitchen. Only down by the floor did a tiny amount of untainted air remain.

Through the haze that now filled the room Stephen saw Al and Antonio still trying to force their way out. Al was bashing away at the shutters with a broken bench; Antonio pounded on the door. The smoke was getting to both of them. Tears and a racking cough weakened their struggles. "If we don't get out of here soon, we've had it!" Uncle Richard muttered.

Stephen watched his uncle's eyes. They glanced around the room, then seemed to go sightless. Stephen knew that look. The wheels were turning in Uncle Richard's head.

Suddenly the eyes were alert again. "Stay down," Uncle Richard said, leaping on top of a table into the worst of the smoke.

The noise turned Antonio and Al around. They gaped as Uncle Richard stood on the table, pulling out his machete.

He sliced once, twice, into the thatched roof above his head. Then he bent down and sucked in some fresh air. "Over here," he said hoarsely.

Al and Antonio scuttled to the table while Uncle Richard took more swings at the thatch. He looked as if he were about to topple off the table, when a big square of roof fell in. Late afternoon sunshine poured in the hole. Smoke poured out.

"Up here!" Uncle Richard gasped. Al was the first up. Uncle Richard laced his hands together to give her a boost up, but the smoke had weakened him. He couldn't support her weight. Stephen had to help boost her out the hole. Next went the wobbly Antonio. "You next," Uncle Richard said to Stephen.

"But how will you get out?" Stephen asked.

"I'll take care of myself," Uncle Richard answered. He picked up the machete from the tabletop and tried to put it into its sheath. It took him three tries.

"That does it," Stephen said. He jumped down to the floor as Uncle Richard yelled after him.

"Get back up here!" Grabbing a bench, Stephen

threw it on the tabletop. Then he clambered up after it.

"We'll go together!" he shouted. "Up on top of this!"

Even standing on the bench they were short of the roof. "Al! We need some help!" Stephen yelled.

Al's face appeared in the hole in the roof. With her pulling on Uncle Richard's rifle sling and Stephen pushing from the bottom, they managed to get him into the fresh air. Then Stephen leaped up. The bench fell down beneath him, but he got high enough to grab the edge of the roof and scramble to safety.

Up in the fresh air the effects of the smoke wore off in moments.

"*Whooof!*" said Uncle Richard, unholstering his pistol. "Let's go have a word with Maria and that old man." He crawled up higher on the roof and scanned the town.

"No sign of anybody," he said. From his vantage point he even got a good look down the trail into the jungle. What he saw there made him stiffen. "The bandits!" he hissed. "We got suckered right into an ambush."

Stephen took a quick peek. The trail was covered with men on mules. He could even hear the jingle of reins drifting into the silent town.

The four of them slid down the roof to the street. A quick search showed no one in town. "The town with no people," Uncle Richard grunted. "And I can guess why. Maria and company intended to leave us unconscious or dead for the bandits to pick up, and they didn't want to be around themselves.''

"I can't believe it!" Antonio said. "They know I work with Le Vac! I'm too important for them to kill me along with you!"

"Dream on," Uncle Richard said. "We've got to get out of here."

That was when they realized the ferryboat was no longer bobbing in the water.

Uncle Richard squinted into the setting sun. "The townspeople must have taken the boat downriver," he said. "We're trapped here."

Stephen looked at the river. "Is there any other way across?"

"In English, you would call this the Dangerous River," Al said. "It has quicksands, trick currents, and then there are the caimans."

"What are caimans?" Stephen asked.

"They're sort of like alligators . . ." Uncle Richard said.

"Wonderful," Stephen said. "And those bandits are going to be here any second. What do we do?"

Uncle Richard patted one of the logs piled against the unfinished part of the cabin. "We ride across on one of these. Come on, let's get it into the water."

The sound of jingling reins got everyone working quickly. Heaving and grunting, they pushed the log to the riverbank.

"You are *loco*—crazy-mad!" Antonio panted as he pushed. "We'll drown before we get halfway across!"

"I'll take my chances with the river rather than with your friends," Uncle Richard said. The log splashed into the water, and he picked up two planks. "Paddles," he said. "And cheer up, Antonio. You're not going with us."

"You mean I am free to go?"

"There are enough dangerous reptiles out there without bringing a snake like you along." Uncle Richard jerked his thumb at the trail. "Move it!" he said.

Antonio ran through the clearing along the trail. The cabin hid him from sight, but they could hear his footsteps. Suddenly he stopped. "Antonio!" one of the bandits called.

"They're in town already!" Al hissed.

Uncle Richard leaped onto the floating log. They all heard Antonio shout, "Le Vac! What are you trying to do? Cheat a partner? Your friends here nearly killed me!"

Stephen gingerly straddled the log. It bobbed in the water, wetting him up to his thighs.

"Don't think about falling," Al said, jumping on behind and putting her paddle into the water. "Just hold tight."

In the background Antonio was still arguing with a gruff-voiced stranger.

"It's a shame my friends didn't do a better job," the gruff voice said. "We can fix that." A shot rang out, followed by a strangled scream.

"Does that mean what I think it does?" Stephen asked.

Uncle Richard dipped his paddle into the water. "They didn't want him back." He looked at Stephen's face. "These guys aren't boy scouts. Especially this Le Vac character. Now, let's get this thing moving."

Stephen clamped his hands and knees to the log as Uncle Richard and Al began paddling. They hit the river current, and were swept out. Stephen glanced over his shoulder. He had a clear view down the trail. A mass of mounted men stood around a huddled figure lying in the dirt. Then two of the bandits looked up, and right at Stephen.

7

JAWS OF DANGER

SATURDAY; 7:56 P.M., *San Bernardo*

It was like a cavalry charge in a western movie. The
bandits swarmed down the trail and onto the riverbank,
howling and waving their weapons. Some held torches
in the gathering dusk. Shots rang out. Uncle Richard
paddled faster. "Move it!" he shouted.

Stephen hunched over the log, and turned his eyes
to the river. "There's another log," he said. "But
how can it go against the current?"

The log opened its mouth, showing Stephen a row
of sharp teeth. "A-a-alligator!" he yelled. His grip
on the log loosened, and he fell sideways into the
river.

Coughing, and thrashing in the water, Stephen
grabbed for the log. Uncle Richard stuck out his
paddle. Stephen snatched it. The alligator sped up to

snatch Stephen. Uncle Richard went for his gun, but there was no time. Stephen, left with the plank in his hands, brought it down with all his strength on the alligator's snout.

Thwack! The alligator blinked in surprise and backed off. Uncle Richard pulled Stephen onto the log. "Steve, you amaze me," he said. "I'd never have thought that would work."

Stephen didn't say anything.

The sky grew dark surprisingly fast. "That's the problem with tropical sunsets," Uncle Richard said. "It's like somebody just turns the sun off."

They kept paddling. Suddenly a loud whack nearly overturned the log.

"That rotten alligator hasn't given up!" Al said, whipping out her gun. The flash of two pistol shots cut the darkness. "What the—" she said. "I think the bullets just bounce off him!"

"Thick hide," Uncle Richard muttered. He thrust the paddle into Stephen's hands. "Hold on to this. I'll have to use the rifle."

Uncle Richard got the beast in his sights. Stephen was nearly deafened by the rifle's roar. While they struggled to keep the log from rolling, they heard a loud bellow. "You got him!" Stephen crowed.

The river was quiet. But suddenly the alligator's tail lashed out of the darkness. "Watch out! We're still not done with him!" Uncle Richard shouted as chunks of log flew up.

The rifle crashed again. Another bellow came from the alligator, but it was much weaker. It didn't follow as they paddled away. "Next stop, the shore," Uncle Richard said.

The three of them nearly fell off the log when they reached the riverbank. Stephen threw himself on the ground. "No stopping yet," Uncle Richard said. "It's only a few more miles to the mine. I don't want those bandits cutting us off."

"A few more miles," Stephen muttered. "So what if my legs fall off?" He got to his feet painfully, following Uncle Richard and Al.

If the day's marching was bad, slogging along in the dark was a nightmare. Branches that Stephen would have seen in daylight kept smacking him in the face. Roots tripped him. He lost count of how many times he fell.

Finally he couldn't get up. He lay in the muck, spitting the foul-tasting gunk from his mouth. "He's gone as far as he can," Al's voice floated out of the dark.

"Not far enough," came Uncle Richard's voice. A pair of hands gently picked him up. "Come on, sport, just a little farther."

They marched on, slower since Uncle Richard was carrying Stephen. All Stephen noticed were the bugs that attacked him. They seemed much more blood-thirsty than their daytime cousins. He fell asleep before they left the jungle, and never felt Uncle Richard put him down by the side of the trail.

But he felt as if he'd only had five minutes sleep when a hand started shaking him.

"G'way, Mom," Stephen mumbled. "I don't feel too good."

The shaking didn't stop. "Stephen, Stephen, get up." It was Al.

"It's still dark," Stephen complained.

Uncle Richard knelt over Stephen and pressed a can and a spoon into his hand. "Get up, Steve. Time for breakfast." He looked at the glowing numerals on his watch. It was 5:07.

Stephen tasted the first mouthful. "Oh, goody. More corned beef hash." He chewed while Uncle Richard talked.

"We're lucky we had time to sleep with those bandits on our tails. But that ferryboat couldn't carry men *and* mules. They'd have to go miles downstream to find a bridge. Now it's time for us to go if we want to reach the mine by daylight. We've really got to keep to this schedule."

Who is he kidding with this schedule stuff? Stephen thought. But he kept quiet and ate.

They finished their meal and started marching up the trail. It began to twist, turn, and climb. The world stopped being black and took on shades of gray. Stephen realized the trail was taking them up into mountains.

The grays got lighter, and they could see the trail winding around the slopes behind them. They could also see a troop of riders galloping along the trail.

"Come on!" Uncle Richard picked up the pace. They trotted along as the trail led them down into a narrow valley. On one side stood a mountain. The other side sloped up gently for about thirty feet, then turned into a sheer cliff.

The clatter of hooves echoed behind them as Uncle Richard broke into a mad dash. "Can't stay on the trail," he said. "They'll just run us down." They left the trail and started climbing.

The higher they went, the steeper the climb became. They soon reached the base of the cliff. Behind them a small army of men on mules charged into the valley.

A small ledge jutted out from the base of the cliff. The three of them piled into the cover it offered.

"Just five more minutes," Uncle Richard muttered.

"What are you saying?" Stephen asked.

"This trail has been zigzagging higher and higher into the mountains." Uncle Richard pointed down at the road. "It makes another sharp turn a little farther on, then cuts back above us, climbing up this cliff face."

The cliff loomed above them. But when Stephen looked off to the side, he could see a series of ledges high up on the wall connected by a steep little track.

"Even their mules couldn't climb that," Uncle Richard said. "They'd have to turn back and find another route." He let out a sigh of annoyance. "But it's no use to us now."

"Why not?" Al asked.

"Haven't you looked at this ledge? It's a dead end." The cliff face above was a straight sheet of rock.

"So the only way out is going back down to the trail," Stephen said. He looked down and saw the bandits milling around on the road below.

A bullet zipped by. "They're shooting at us!" Stephen said.

"They just want to get our attention."

"They got mine," said Al.

A heavyset, bearded bandit shouted up to them. "Duffy! I want to talk to you!"

"That must be Paul Le Vac," Uncle Richard said.

The bandit sat on his mule, a cigar jutting out of his mouth. "You can't fight all of us, you know." He struck a match on the seat of his pants and used it to light his cigar. "Join us and I'll make you a partner."

"I don't like what happened to your last partner," Uncle Richard shouted back.

Le Vac reached into his saddlebag and pulled out a package. He touched his cigar to it. "Have it your way!" he shouted, hurling the package up to the ledge.

It was a bundle of waxy sticks with a burning fuse sticking out. "Dynamite!" Stephen yelled as it bounced across the rock toward them.

Uncle Richard grabbed the bomb and lobbed it away from them at the base of the cliff. "Actually I think it's gelignite."

The sticks went off with a roar. Cracks shot through the whole cliff face. Then it came tumbling down. As the rocks crashed, Uncle Richard went on talking. "Yes. Much more powerful than dynamite."

The dust cleared away. "You're pretty good, Duffy," Le Vac called. "But the next bomb will have a shorter fuse."

Uncle Richard studied the cliff face. "Their plan backfired," he said. "That gelignite blasted a new path up the cliff for us." He took Al by the arm. "Look at these rocks over on our left. Could you and Steve climb them to get to the ledge above?"

Al looked at the new, craggier cliff. "I suppose we could—but those *bandidos* down there aren't going to sit on their hands while we do it!"

Uncle Richard had already turned to scan the mountainside covered with bandits. Then he started to push buttons on his watch.

"What are you doing?" Stephen asked.

"Figuring out some probable rockslide routes," Uncle Richard answered. He looked at his answers, nodded, and unslung the rifle from his shoulder. "When I shoot, run like the devil."

He squeezed the trigger and his single shot hit a rock. But when that rock started to roll, it brought half the mountaintop with it. The bandits dashed down the slope out of the rock's path and into the road.

Al and Stephen raced along the ledge, then jumped for the rocks Uncle Richard had pointed out. Al grabbed Stephen's hand and hauled him up. "Come on," she said. "This isn't going to last forever!"

They were on the cliff face before the bandits even saw them. But they were too busy dodging rocks to shoot.

Stephen and Al panted as they pulled themselves from handhold to handhold. The way to the ledges was a lot harder than it had looked. "People do this for fun?" he said.

Le Vac's voice cut through the morning air as he reorganized his forces. Bandits began climbing after them.

"Got to climb faster," Al said, wheezing as she grabbed onto a small boulder. It came loose in her hand. *"Madre mia!"* she cried. Stephen looked up to see her totter back. He pushed himself up and seized hold of her leg. "I've got you!" he said.

Al couldn't steady herself. She tried to push forward to the cliff face, but only teetered back. More and more of her weight came onto Stephen's arm. The extra weight made his footholds crumble.

"Hold on," he muttered, trying to brace himself. One foot slipped out into nothingness. The other felt the rock beneath it disintegrate. They slid for an instant, then his pants caught on a jutting stone. It tore a big hole at his knee, but slowed them down. "Mom's gonna kill me," he said. They started sliding again. "Guess I don't have to worry about that."

Suddenly he jerked to a stop. A hand seized hold of his belt. "Hope you buckled this good and tight," Uncle Richard said, yanking both of them onto a ledge.

Back on solid ground, Al stood and shuddered. Uncle Richard took her arm. "Are you okay?"

Stephen caught a glimpse of motion at his feet. He looked down to see a hat and a rifle pushing over the edge. Then a nose and a pair of eyes appeared. Stephen and the bandit stared at each other in shock.

8

BIG PROBLEMS

SUNDAY; 5:48 A.M., *San Bernardo*

Frantically Stephen fumbled in his knapsack for a weapon. All he could find was a can of corned beef hash. He wound up and threw it at the crown of the hat.

"*Yow!*" the bandit yelled. His hands went to his head. They should have been holding on to the rocks. "*Oh, nooooo!*" he cried as he slid down the cliff face.

Stephen looked down. "He was lucky," he said. "He landed on some friends." The bandits shook their fists at the ledge.

The climbing got easier when they reached the trail. In moments Uncle Richard pulled them to the top of the cliff. They looked down to see what the bandits were doing. "They're scattering from the bottom of the cliff,'' Uncle Richard said. ''Why?''

His eyes widened and his jaw dropped. ''Move it!'' he said.

They raced away from the edge. ''What-what's up?'' Al gasped.

''Gelignite . . . trying to blast . . . *whole cliff?*'' All three poured on speed. Al pulled into the lead as Uncle Richard reached back to Stephen.

The whole world seemed to leap upward. Stephen fell to the ground. As he pushed himself up, cracks appeared in the cliff around him.

Uncle Richard was on his knees, swaying dizzily. He held his head, trying to shake it. Stephen ran to his uncle and grabbed his hand. Uncle Richard got to his feet and they dashed desperately for safety.

A crevice gaped open before them. Al stood on the other side. ''Come on! It's safe here!''

The rock beneath them slipped down. Uncle Richard's hand tightened. ''*Jump!*'' he said. They cleared the crevice and landed on solid ground just as the section they'd left crashed down.

Stephen stared at that empty spot for a moment. Uncle Richard shook him. ''Not healthy to keep thinking about that,'' he said. ''Besides, we've got to get going.''

The top of the cliff formed a ridgeline, and a few more minutes of climbing brought them to the lip of a bowl-shaped valley. Stephen knelt there, looking down. ''So that's what a gold mine looks like,'' he said. "A wooden shack and a big hole in a mountain. Not very impressive."

Uncle Richard knelt beside him. "Not what you expected, is it? But you can't see the best part—the cable car system. We use it to ship the ore across to the next mountain. That's where the train from Puerto Escobar comes in—" He broke off, looking at his watch. "We're just about on schedule in spite of that delay in the mountains. Let's get down to the mine. At least there are no guards"—the door to the shack slammed open and a man lumbered out—"except for that one."

The man had a long, dirty black beard. To Stephen's eyes, all his clothes seemed too small. The man stretched in the sunshine, then scratched himself. Finally he turned to go back inside. He stepped into the shack—and hit his forehead smack on the top of the doorway. Even at the top of the valley they could hear his yell. Then he hauled off and kicked the door. One of the hinges broke, and the door hung lopsided.

"I hope that's a very small, cheaply built shack," Al breathed.

"Unh-uh. That's a very large, strong man," Uncle Richard said. They watched the giant pace around outside the shack, rubbing his forehead. "But he doesn't seem too bright." He stood up. "I'm going to try something," he said, and walked down to the mine.

When Uncle Richard got near the shack, the giant stopped rubbing his head and went for his gun. He was so busy with Uncle Richard, he never noticed the other two figures furtively scrambling down. Stephen and Al got behind a rock just in time to hear Uncle Richard speak.

"Hello, hello," he said. "Is Mr. Le Vac around? I'm sure he must be expecting me." He stood in front of the giant and smiled.

"My gosh!" Stephen said. "He barely comes up to that guy's chest!"

The giant blinked and opened his mouth a few times. Uncle Richard looked inside the shack. "No one else around, eh? This is very disappointing. Are you sure he didn't leave a message for me?"

"He didn't say nothing about no one coming," the giant said, holstering his gun. "He said take care of anybody who came here." His arms whipped around Uncle Richard in a crushing bear hug.

Al raised her pistol, then put it down. "Blast!" she said to Stephen. "I can't get a clear shot at him!"

"You're making a terrible mistake," Uncle Richard said, wheezing as the giant tightened his arms.

"Yuh. We'll talk to Mr. Le Vac about it." The giant loosened his arm a bit, so he could take Uncle Richard's guns away.

"You know, you're beginning to get me very angry." Uncle Richard looked up into the giant's face.

The giant dumped him on the ground in a heap. "What are you going to do about it, little man?"

"This," Uncle Richard said, kicking the giant in the knee.

"*Ooooooooooooooey!*" yelled the giant. He bent over to grab his knee. Uncle Richard reached up and dug his hands into the giant's shoulder. The huge man froze into a weird statue.

Looking over his shoulder, Uncle Richard called, "Are you going to stay up there all day? Move it!"

"What did you do to that guy?" Al asked as she came up to Uncle Richard.

"It's a jujitsu trick," he explained. "As long as I hold him, he's paralyzed."

"That's really neat."

"It would be neater if you found something to tie him up with. I can't hold him like this forever."

Stephen found some baling wire in the shack, and Al wrapped it around the giant's hands and feet. "That should take care of laughing boy," Uncle Richard said. "Now, into the office. I want to check out the maps of the mine."

The inside of the office was a shambles. "Well, you could guess he wouldn't be a good housekeeper." Uncle Richard went over to a large colored map on the wall and ran his finger over it. "Here's the new shaft." He ran his finger down. "Here's a note. Shows where they found the old tunnels." He started tearing the map off the wall.

"What are you doing?" Al said.

"Le Vac and company might know the mine by now, but why should I make it easy for them? If anybody comes after us, we'll lose them in the mine.

And I hope they *stay* lost." He tore the map to shreds, then headed to the doorway. Halfway out, he stopped and grabbed three miner's helmets from a rack by the door. "I have a feeling we'll need these."

"I think you're right," Al said, pointing. "Look up there!"

Men came running down onto the valley floor, shouting.

"Their walk around the mountain must have made them cranky," Uncle Richard said.

A few shots whizzed past them as Uncle Richard led the way to the shaft. He stopped for a moment to fiddle with the lamps on the helmets. One came on, throwing a beam of light through the darkness. Then the other two lamps were shining too. "Let's lose these nuts in the mine!"

Stephen's stomach growled at the mention of nuts. What a time to start thinking about Mom's health-food store!

They ran along mine tunnels, their helmet beams casting weird shadows on the walls. Voices and footfalls followed them as the bandits entered the shaft.

"Duffy!" Le Vac's voice echoed down the galleries. "You think you were smart getting into the mine? How are you going to get out?"

Stephen stopped short. "How *do* we get out?" he asked.

"Don't worry about it," Uncle Richard said, heading deeper into the shafts. "I have a plan."

"Where have I heard that before?" Stephen asked.

He turned to follow Uncle Richard, but something crunched behind him.

Stephen whirled, and a man appeared in the light from his helmet. It was Le Vac. Stephen whipped around and streaked down the tunnel, running for his life.

His quick glimpse of Le Vac had shown him exactly what kind of man they were dealing with. He didn't look too bad from far away, Stephen thought. But up close . . . that face—*brrrr!* Stephen had seen lots of movie bad guys, and they had hard faces, but Le Vac's face said pure evil. From the squinty eyes to the tight mouth it was the face of a dangerous man. But the final, gruesome touch was the dead-white scar that ran from the corner of his right eye, down past the edge of his mouth, to end in his chin. Not even his bushy black beard could hide it. The scar alone gave Stephen extra speed.

That was just as well, since Le Vac was right behind him. "Here they are! Get them! A hundred American dollars for each head!" With a cheer, the bandits came speeding down the tunnels.

The rock walls whipped past as Stephen ran.

"A hundred dollars? That's all we're worth?" Al panted as Stephen caught up with her.

"We'll be worth a lot less if we don't get out of here."

Three tunnel entrances stretched before them. Without breaking stride Uncle Richard led them into the right-hand one. Behind them came the sounds of the pursuing bandits, but there seemed to be fewer of them.

"The rest are checking out the side tunnels," Uncle Richard said, running along. "Good!" He stopped at a pit cut into the tunnel floor. A ladder went down into the hole. Stephen leaned over the edge, but his light didn't penetrate to the bottom. Uncle Richard nudged him onto the ladder. "Move it!" he said. They could hear footsteps coming closer.

The climb down seemed to last forever. "Uncle Richard, where is this leading us?" Stephen whispered.

"It goes to the old tunnels."

Stephen halted his descent. "The old tunnels?"

Uncle Richard's foot nearly landed on Stephen's hand. "I said, move it, Steve. The bandits won't be so eager to follow us there."

"Yeah, a wonderful, safe place—filled with death-traps!" Al's voice came from overhead.

"If you don't get going, this ladder will be a deathtrap." Light appeared at the mouth of the pit above. "The bandits!" Uncle Richard hissed.

Stephen started down the ladder again, leaping from rung to rung. But by the time they reached the bottom of the pit, he could see a ring of miner's helmets—and faces—up at the top. The bandits made a lot of noise, as if they were trying to work up the nerve to keep up the chase. One bandit raised his rifle, but another knocked it away. "Fool! Do you want the ceiling to cave in?"

"Then how do we get them?" the first bandit

asked. His friend pulled a long, shiny knife from his belt.

"This is what we use to get them!" he yelled, jumping onto the ladder.

Uncle Richard yanked something out of his knapsack.

"That's the flare gun from my plane!" Al said. "Don't you think we're a bit deep to try signaling for help?"

"It'll discourage those clowns for a little while." Uncle Richard fit a flare shell into the gun, then aimed it upward. "Don't look up."

He fired the flare. The tall shaft filled with blinding light. The walls echoed the screams of the bandits as they fell over each other, yelling, "Watch out! Watch out!"

Uncle Richard knelt by a jagged hole in the floor of the shaft, shining a flashlight through. More tunnels—smaller ones. Dust was thick on the floors, and the wooden beams holding up the roof were black with age. Uncle Richard eased through the hole. Then he gave Al a hand down. Finally it was Stephen's turn. The musty air made him sneeze. He had a terrible feeling that this place would *not* be good for his health.

9

BALANCING ACT

SUNDAY; 8:09 A.M., *San Bernardo*

"I think we've lost them," Uncle Richard whispered as he led the way through the cramped tunnels. "We've passed so many turnoffs, they can only guess about our trail."

"I'd like to put more distance between us and them," Al said from her rear-guard position. "Can't you speed it up a little?"

"Sure, if you want to set off a nice booby trap." Uncle Richard flashed his light over the tunnel walls and floor, looking intently. He shook his head. "I don't understand it. We should've hit a trap by now." Uncle Richard stepped past a big crack in the wall. "All clear," he said.

Then the ax fell.

All Stephen saw was a blur. Not until the ax

thudded into the ground did he realize he'd almost been sliced in two. He froze, staring at the six inches of heavy steel axhead sticking out of the floor. Al came up and nearly tripped over him.

"*Ooof!*" she said. "What do you think you're trying to—" She grew quiet as her beam picked up the ax. Uncle Richard knelt to examine it.

"Here's what set it off," he said, pointing to an old wire on the floor. "The machinery is so old and rusty, it must have jammed for a second. Good thing you weren't right on my heels."

"N-n-n-no k-k-k-kidding," Stephen said.

"I always thought the idea was to find the traps before they went off," Al said.

"Very funny," Uncle Richard said.

They made their way deeper into the tunnels. Stephen noticed that the wooden supports disappeared, and the walls became more irregular. Uncle Richard flashed his light around. "I think we're in a natural cave."

From the darkness ahead they heard a rushing, bubbling sound. "What can that be?" Al asked.

"Sounds like water," Uncle Richard replied. "An underground stream maybe. We never had any water problems in the new mine, but this isn't the new mine . . ." He stopped as the tunnel opened out into a big cave. Running through the middle of it was a broad stream, wider than they could jump. A stone bridge ran from where they stood all the way across to an opening in the far wall of the cavern. A little rocky island in the middle of the stream held up the bridge.

Uncle Richard knelt by the bridge, examining it. "I think this whole thing is made from one piece of stone. Now, why would they do that?"

"Maybe they built to last," Al said. "This bridge looks like it's been here forever. See how much green gunk has grown up on it? And look at the far side there—those big rock spear things hanging down—stalag . . ."

"Stalactites," Stephen said.

"Thanks for the geology lesson, kid. Can you tell how long they've been there?"

"Not really. I just started collecting rocks and reading a little about them."

Uncle Richard shone his light on the stalactites. "Look at that," he said. "They've grown so far, they're actually touching the bridge."

Sounds came roaring down the tunnel; the bandits were shouting loudly. "Seems like our friends are getting warm," Uncle Richard said. He stepped onto the bridge.

Stephen followed, then Al. They shuffled slowly along, careful of the green slime that coated the rock.

Stephen stopped. "Does anyone hear a creaking sound?"

Uncle Richard stopped too. "You're right."

"Is it my imagination," Al said, "or do you feel the bridge—uh—moving?"

"It's tilting!" shouted Stephen.

"No wonder this bridge was built in one piece!"

Uncle Richard said. "It's a giant seesaw balanced on that island in the middle of the stream. The end we're standing on is going down. It's trying to dump us into the river." They looked at the water hissing beneath them.

"Why hasn't it dumped us all the way?" Al asked.

"The bridge is caught on those stalactites you noticed," Uncle Richard said. "We're okay for as long as they hold. But we've got to get ourselves somewhere safe," he said, shuffling along as fast as he could.

"Where is someplace safe?" Stephen asked.

"The center of the bridge," Uncle Richard answered. "Remember? Like a seesaw. Sit out on the ends, and you make it tilt. Sit in the middle, and the seesaw stays level."

They were almost at the middle when Al slipped. *"Yiiiiiiii!"* she cried as her feet flew up into the air. Her fall was followed by an ominous *snap!* from the far end of the bridge.

"There go the stalactites," Uncle Richard said. The bridge began to tilt crazily. He hurled himself forward, sliding along the slimy mosses covering the stone. The bridge moved level again as his weight landed on the far side of the balance point.

"Steve, move until you're right in the middle." Crawling slowly, Stephen did as he was told. The bridge rocked only a little.

"Okay, Al and I will move in. If we go slowly, we should stay balanced." They crept along until all of them were kneeling at the center of the bridge.

"This is great, but how are we going to get off?" Stephen asked.

"Uncle Richard thought for a minute. "It's going to be a heck of a balancing act, but here's how we can do it—" He turned to his watch. "I weigh 172. Steve?"

"I'm 104 pounds."

Uncle Richard turned to Al.

"One hundred and five," she said. Uncle Richard kept looking at her. "All right, 120!"

He nodded at his watch. "If you two go out eighteen feet along the bridge, you'll balance me so I can get across."

"It's a shame I didn't bring my ruler with me," said Al.

"I'll tell you when to stop," Uncle Richard said.

Moments later Uncle Richard had inched along the bridge toward the tunnel opening on the far end. Al and Stephen balanced him by crawling back the way they'd come. "Great plan," Al snorted as she crawled. "If we live through this, we can all join the circus."

The balancing act worked. Al and Stephen together weighed more than Uncle Richard. By the time they were three-quarters of the way back, he'd reached the far end of the bridge. "No traps here," he said. Then he swept up all the broken parts of the stalactites with his arms. "Now comes the tricky part. If I can get off the bridge while making up for my weight with these rocks . . ."

Finally he stood on solid ground at the far end of

the bridge. "Did it! And we're still balanced! Let me get some more rocks, and we'll get Al over."

Al crawled over while Uncle Richard used rocks and Stephen to balance the bridge for her. It ended with Stephen at the beginning of the bridge and Al at the end. "That leaves you, Steve. Let me get things ready for you."

Stephen started crawling while Uncle Richard moved the rocks. When he got to the middle of the bridge, he stopped. "Hey, wait a second!" he said. "There's nobody back there to balance me! How do I get across?"

"Don't worry about it." Uncle Richard jammed rocks under the bridge. "You're very light, so the bridge won't move so quickly. And even if the bridge does tilt, we'll be here to catch you."

"Even if the bridge does tilt . . . ?" Stephen cried.

Slowly he started crawling across the bridge. He felt it sway, grinding away at the rocks jammed under it.

"Move it, Steve," Uncle Richard said. His eyes were fixed on the mouth of the tunnel at the far end of the bridge. Then Stephen heard voices behind him.

"What's that?" "A bridge!" "There they are!" "Get them!" Bandits—right in the tunnel!

"If they hit this bridge while I'm still on it," Stephen said, "*boing!*"

He scuttled along the slimy surface as fast as he could. The end of the bridge was just out of reach when Al yelled, "Jump!"

Behind him one of the bandits shouted, "Me first!" He leaped onto the bridge just as Stephen tried to jump off. The seesaw turned into a diving board. It flipped Stephen high into the air. He watched in horror as he flew up at the spearlike stalactites on the ceiling. The tip of one came within inches of his head, then pulled away as he started to fall.

The rushing waters bubbled below him. Push forward! Stephen thought. But push against what? Air? Everything went into slow motion as he spun around. The ground was still too far away, and the water came swirling nearer. . . .

10

STEP ON A CRACK . . .

SUNDAY; 9:57 A.M., *San Bernardo*

Arms wrapped around Stephen, pulling him back. His eyes shot open, and found themselves staring into Al's. "How?" Stephen said. Then he saw how. Uncle Richard stood braced against a rock as he held on to Al. She was leaning far out over the water. "Good catch, huh?" she grinned.

Uncle Richard yanked them both in, and they all ran down the tunnel. "I almost wish we could see how those idiots handle that bridge," he said.

From the yelling and splashing, it didn't seem that the bandits were handling it well at all.

Tunnel walls closed in on them again. They came to a fork, then another one. Each time, Uncle Richard picked the right-hand tunnel. Then they hit a blind tunnel and had to retrace their steps. The other tunnel took a sharp turn and ended in a room so large the light from their helmets couldn't reach to the far wall.

What they could see reminded Stephen of a castle they'd once seen in Scotland. These walls were made of square stone blocks. Above them stretched a ceiling of carved metal plates. But the light of their lamps really showed off the floor. It seemed to go on forever, huge blood-red square tiles with black cracks around them.

"This must have been a feasting hall or something like that," Al said. "We've really made it into Mad Jack's fortress." She stepped into the hall, but Uncle Richard yanked her back.

"No place else in the mine has these tiles," he said. "I don't like it. Put a little weight on them, and you might trigger something off."

Al jerked around and stared at him. "Well, what are we supposed to do? Stand around and wonder about them?"

Uncle Richard unloaded his rifle. "We test them out first."

He leaned over the floor and tapped one of the tiles. Nothing happened. He moved onto the safe tile and tapped another one, and another, working his way out across the floor. "Step only on the tiles I tested."

"If this isn't the stupidest thing I ever saw," Al said as they slowly moved across the room. "It will take forever . . . and you're the one who's always saying 'Move it.' "

Uncle Richard pretended not to hear her. He just kept hitting tiles with the rifle butt. Finally he straightened up, rubbing his back. His foot landed square on a crack between two tiles.

"Look out!" Al yelled.

Uncle Richard jumped back just in time. One of the heavy metal plates from the ceiling smashed down where he'd been standing. It missed, but in dodging it Uncle Richard set off several more plates. He had a hot couple of minutes before he finally stood on a safe tile.

"What made that happen?" Stephen asked.

Uncle Richard breathed heavily. "It's almost funny. I was worrying about the tiles, but it's the cracks." He knelt down and gently put his hand on one of them. It wasn't really a crack at all. The spaces between the tiles were filled with a gummy black substance. "I don't know what it is," Uncle Richard said, "but there's some sort of trigger hidden under it."

They walked carefully across the floor, making sure their feet touched only tiles. The old saying kept running through Stephen's mind, with a twist: Step on a crack . . . break your *own* back!

The lamps on their helmets showed them the far wall of the hall—and the exit tunnel. All three speeded up a little. Al put her foot on a tile—and another metal plate came flying down!

Uncle Richard swept her out of the way as the plate shattered on the floor. "But I—I didn't step on the crack," Al said.

"You sure?"

"Of course I'm sure! Do you think I'm stupid enough to go clomping on one of those cracks when I know what will happen?"

"Two possible explanations," Uncle Richard said, unslinging his rifle. "The machinery went wrong—and could go wrong again."

Al and Stephen glanced up at the ceiling.

"Or it's a new kind of trap. Maybe Mad Jack suspected that people would figure out the cracks so he set up some of the tiles to trigger the plates too."

He leaned over and rapped the tile in front of him with the rifle. Then he shot a look at the ceiling. He hit the next tile and looked up again. This time Al had nothing to say.

Uncle Richard tested his way across the floor, and Al and Stephen followed him carefully. Their leg muscles ached from placing their feet so precisely. Their eyes kept darting from the floor to the ceiling above.

At last they could see the rocky tunnel floor just a short distance ahead of them. There were only three more tiles to cross. Then there were two. Uncle Richard stopped the march while he checked for any other traps. Finally they stood on solid rock again. "I'll never trust another tile floor," Stephen said. He was surprised to realize that he'd been holding his breath.

They walked along the new tunnel, working the cramps out of their legs. The tunnel made a sharp turn to the left. A few yards later it made a sharp turn to the right. Uncle Richard kept them back while he took a quick look around the corners. "There's no reason for a tunnel to start wiggling like this," he said, "unless it's to catch somebody off-guard."

"Maybe men were supposed to wait here to ambush people," Al said.

Uncle Richard shone his light around. "At least there are no traps."

They went through the turns and found themselves in a straight tunnel again. They followed it slowly. Their lights picked up an opening in the right-hand wall.

"A new tunnel?" Stephen asked.

They looked in. It wasn't a new tunnel. It was a doorway. Beyond was a small room carved out of the rock. The first thing Stephen saw were words scratched into the wall. The second thing he saw was a skeleton.

11

"IF STONE COULD SPEAK . . ."

SUNDAY; 11:02 A.M., *San Bernardo*

Pictures covered the walls, a rug was spread out over the floor, and heavily carved wooden furniture stood all around. Once the chamber must have been splendid. But that was a long time ago. Now everything was eaten away or covered in dust.

The skeleton sprawled in what was left of a huge chair—a throne, almost. Tatters of cloth clung to the bones. Under the grayness of the dust Stephen could see that the cloth had once been red velvet.

"They say Mad Jack always wore red velvet," Al said softly.

Uncle Richard stepped around the skeleton to look at the message on the wall. "Looks like Mad Jack—if that's who we have here—tore down this tapestry to expose the rock. Then he chipped away at the wall to leave that message."

Stephen looked down at the floor. A rusted dagger lay beside the skeleton's hand.

"He was a hard worker, but a rotten poet," Uncle Richard said, reading the message on the wall.

> *Searchers, if the stone could speak*
> *ye would find the thing ye seek.*

"That *must* be Jenson there," Al said. "That's a madman's message, for sure." Her eyes glowed. "If he's here, so is the crown!" She started searching among the moldy finery in the room. By the time she was done, clouds of dust filled the chamber, and most of the furniture was piled in one corner. She even moved Mad Jack and his throne so she could search the place where it had stood.

"Nothing," she snapped. "If this turns out to be some silly, empty legend"—she breathed heavily—"somebody is going to pay!"

"Just like Le Vac wants to pay one hundred dollars for our heads?" Stephen said. "Shouldn't we get out of here?" He turned to Uncle Richard.

But Uncle Richard still stared at the message. " 'Searchers, if the stone could speak . . .' " he said. "Well, there's stone all around us."

"Stone all around us! Right! Right!" Al said. She swept around the room again, taking down pictures and tearing down curtains. Uncle Richard joined her, rapping and tapping at walls.

Stephen stood in the dust, coughing. He stepped into the clearer air of the tunnel. "Somebody better look out for the bandits," he said. "Those two sure won't."

He stood in the entrance to the room as Uncle Richard and Al went around the walls a second time. Then they tore up the rug and tapped around the floor. They even did a little tapping on the ceiling.

"Nothing!" Al said again. "What are we doing wrong? It must be around here!"

Uncle Richard looked at his watch. "We're wasting too much time," he said. "We'd be trapped in here if the bandits came along."

"They've got to get over that bridge and through a bunch of wrong turns and that booby-trapped hall before they get here," Al said. "We just can't give up looking!"

"One more time," Uncle Richard said. They began thumping and bumping again.

Stephen sat down in the tunnel, looking over a pile of old stones Al had thrown out of the chamber. "Hey, there are some nice quartz crystals in these," Stephen said.

Al's voice floated into the tunnel. "We're looking for a treasure, and he's looking at rocks. Rocks in the *head*, I think. . . ."

Annoyed, Stephen kicked a rock away. Then he bent to pick it up. It was a little larger than a football and had nothing interesting about it, not even any crystals. Stephen weighed it in his hands. "In fact, it's not quartz at all. Hey . . ."

He rushed back into the chamber. Uncle Richard and Al both had their eyes glued to the wall as they tapped. "Hey," Stephen said again.

Uncle Richard took a step to the right and started tapping at a new piece of wall. "This isn't the best time for a chat."

"I want you to look at this rock."

Al took a step to the left. "Just what we need. More rocks. I suppose we're not seeing enough rock as it is."

"But . . ."

"Steve." Annoyance crept into Uncle Richard's voice.

"This rock doesn't belong in this mine."

Uncle Richard and Al turned around. "Huh?"

"All the rock around here is quartz. That's what you usually find in a gold mine. But there's hardly any quartz in this rock."

"What is it then?" Al asked.

"That's the really weird thing." Stephen pointed at one side. "Half of it is something called gabbro. It's made when rocks melt from intense heat. The other half is limestone, which is only made under water. The two halves sort of look alike, but there's no way they should be together."

Uncle Richard snatched at the rock, grunting as he held it up for a look.

"Oh, boy!" Al's eyes sparkled. "It's got to be the treasure." She rubbed her hands together.

"What I don't understand is, what good will it do us to find a treasure?" Stephen said.

Al looked at him for a moment with her mouth open. "Are you feeling all right, kid?"

"I mean, I read about something like this not so long ago. Some guys found a treasure on an island down here. But the local government took it all away from them."

"Hey, listen, they don't call San Bernardo the treasure island for nothing," Al said. "The whole island depends on the money treasure hunters bring in. We don't get tourists down here. We get people looking for Jenson's treasures. The government knows that. They passed a special law so that anyone who found a treasure could keep it all—except for a tax."

Uncle Richard held up the rock. "Shine the light just right, and you see a thin crack running down the middle of this stone." He put the rock down on the floor, pressing with his fingers around the stone. "Ah!" *Crack* went the rock, and it split in half.

The crown stuck out of the stone like a golden peach pit, shining dully in the lamplight. They looked at it quietly. Finally Stephen said, "Pretty small, isn't it? Looks like it would just about fit my head."

The crown was no work of art. It looked like someone had taken a bar of gold and hammered away at it until they had a thin doughnut. Then they drilled a few holes and stuck jewels into them.

"It's not what I expected to see," Al said. "But it certainly is a treasure. The jewels alone are worth a fortune!"

"Good," a voice said from behind them.

12

THE KILLER FLOOR AND THE DOOR TO NOWHERE

SUNDAY; 12:38 P.M., *San Bernardo*

They spun around to see a figure leaning against the tunnel wall. It was Le Vac. A machete gleamed in his hand.

He came into the chamber, followed by a group of bandits. An unpleasant smile spread across his scarred face. "Now I get the treasure and I'll pay myself a hundred bucks—for your head." He pointed with his machete at Uncle Richard. "How would you like it? One quick chop? Or a long, slow death?"

Uncle Richard's machete slipped out of its sheath. "It may be longer than you think, handsome," Uncle Richard said.

With a roar Le Vac charged in. His machete *whooshed* through the air as he sliced at Uncle

Richard's head. Uncle Richard met the attack, grasping the handle of his machete in both hands.

He looks like a warrior from a Japanese samurai flick, Stephen said to himself.

Le Vac was a brawler, sweeping away with his oversized cleaver. Yet somehow his blows never landed. Uncle Richard met them with his blade, darting back and forth, slowing the attack up. It's like he's fencing, Stephen thought.

The only problem was, Le Vac had a powerful pair of arms. Every time the machetes clashed, he almost knocked the blade from Uncle Richard's hands.

Slowly Uncle Richard had to retreat. But the chamber didn't give him much room to maneuver. Soon his back was to the junk pile that Al had made. The scar twisted on Le Vac's face as he smiled in triumph. He took a big swing at Uncle Richard. Then his jaw dropped as he missed. His blade whistled into the junk, and smashed Mad Jack's skull right off his body. It bounced around on the floor, looking as if it were laughing.

The bandits had stood in a group at the door, enjoying the show. Now they gaped as Uncle Richard shoved Le Vac off-balance. He tottered back. Uncle Richard went into action. With bold, sweeping moves, his steel threatened Le Vac's head, then his legs, then his arms. The bandit moved frantically, trying to keep his machete between him and a blade that seemed to be everywhere at once. "I've never seen anyone handle a machete like that," someone hissed.

Now Le Vac was backing up, trying to defend himself from Uncle Richard's hacking blade.

When he had Le Vac right up against the crowd of bandits, Uncle Richard darted a look over his shoulder. "Behind me!" he hissed to Stephen and Al.

They ran up as Uncle Richard went into another attack. Stephen couldn't believe it. Uncle Richard's machete seemed to swoop around the bandit's blade, yanking it from his hands. It flew up to land with a *thunk!* in one of the wooden beams in the ceiling.

Uncle Richard's machete looped back. He swung like a baseball player going for a home run. Only when it landed with a loud *thwack!* did Stephen realize that his uncle was using the flat edge of the blade.

It hit Le Vac in the belly. *"Whoooooooooof!"* he said, doubling over. Uncle Richard grabbed him by the neck and hurled him into the crowd of bandits, making a hole in the wall of men.

"Move it," Uncle Richard yelled. Stephen ran right behind him. But the great escape screeched to a halt as they turned back to see what had happened to Al, who was still inside the chamber. The bandits had scrambled to their feet, surrounding her, and from the middle of the mob came a gleam of gold and a heavy thud. One man staggered back. Then Al swung the crown in an uppercut to his chin. The man fell and she leaped over him, running to Stephen and Uncle Richard. "Most expensive brass knuckles in the world," she said.

For a moment the bandits were too surprised to do

anything. Then they were after her like a pack of baying hounds. The escaping trio bounced through the zigzag passages, then ran full speed down a long straight tunnel. Stephen watched the walls fly by. "Wait a minute," he said. "We should have come to the room with the tile floor by now. . . ." He put on more speed to get level with Uncle Richard and Al.

"We're in . . . new tunnel," he wheezed. "Watch out . . . more traps."

He tripped, flopping facedown. As he pushed himself up he saw little holes appearing all over the floor of the tunnel. He jumped to his feet. Things were coming out of the holes. "Snakes?" he asked.

No, these were still and straight and very sharp. "Pointed stakes!" Stephen yelled.

Uncle Richard and Al were ahead of him in the middle of the trap. "Keep going!" Uncle Richard shouted. Al ran a little bit ahead of him, clutching the golden crown.

The stakes sprouted up higher and higher, like some sort of killer plants. First they were only an inch high, then a couple of inches, then six inches, then a foot. Stephen had to jump higher with every step he took. And the stakes were so close together, he had to watch where his feet landed.

Behind them the bandits came blundering onto the stakes. Gruesome screams echoed down the tunnel.

As Stephen ran, his eyes never left the stakes. How high can they get? he asked himself. Then he noticed something—each stake was smeared with a black substance around the point. "Poisoned!"

The stakes seemed to stretch forever down the tunnel. Stephen's breathing grew ragged.

Al was well in the lead by now. "Ahead!" she cried. "It's clear! No stakes!"

The stakes had risen to Stephen's knees. He tried to speed up and his toe thudded against one of them. As he tripped, all Stephen could see were spikes flying up.

"Here!" Out of the corner of his eye Stephen saw Uncle Richard's hand. He grabbed it and pulled himself up. "Just a few more now," Uncle Richard said.

They ran on. The stakes rose higher and higher, Stephen barely clearing the last row. He landed hard and rolled across the floor. Getting to his knees, he looked back at the stakes. They were now higher than a grown man's waist, and still rising.

"That should slow those bandits down for a while," Al said.

"Not for too long," Uncle Richard said, staring down the tunnel. "The stakes are only wood. If they keep their wits about them, the bandits could chop their way through with machetes."

"Let's hope they don't keep their wits about them then," Al said.

Uncle Richard smiled. "At least we can use this time to try and lose them again." He began to run.

At the mention of time Stephen glanced at his watch—and immediately glanced away. "Time is moving so fast," he said, "we'll never get home before Mom and Dad." He raced to catch up to the others.

They had come to another fork in the tunnel. Uncle Richard hit some buttons on his watch and looked at the dial. An arrowhead of light appeared. It went around in a circle, then stopped—an automatic compass.

"That's north," Uncle Richard said. He looked at the two tunnels, and pointed at the one on the left. "I think this one goes in the same direction as the tunnel we came down. It should lead us back."

Al shrugged. "Sounds worth a try."

But Uncle Richard remained standing in front of the tunnels as he said, "Another thing. The last few tunnels we've been in all seem to slant up. If this tunnel goes much higher, I think we'll be even with some of the bottom workings of the new mine." Uncle Richard went back to his watch. This time, numbers flitted across. "I was right. We're 137 feet underground. There may be just a few yards of rock separating the two sets of tunnels."

The tunnel led them to a big room dug out of the stone. Uncle Richard walked in cautiously, shining his light around. The beam caught dozens of wooden supports standing around the room. They threw weird shadows on the walls. It took a moment for Stephen to realize that not all the dark spots on the walls were shadows. "Look at all the tunnel entrances!" he said.

"Seven of them," Uncle Richard said. "This must have been the center of the old mine. The miners brought the gold here"—his light flashed on a pile of moldering leather bags—"then it was transported to the surface."

"Hey!" said Al. "Do you think we could find a way out from here?"

"Possible . . . but not probable," Uncle Richard said. "We never found traces of an old mine before. The entrance probably caved in." He aimed the light at the ceiling of the large room. Stephen noticed that it seemed to sag between the supporting timbers. "Looks like we could have a cave-in here if we're not careful."

They made their way in gently, ducking under the low-hanging support beams. Uncle Richard walked over to one of the tunnels on the opposite wall and shone his light in. Al looked down the one next to it.

"Hey! There's a door here!" They followed her down the tunnel. It ended about thirty feet from the room, in a huge, iron-banded wooden door.

Treasure-hunter's fever burned in Al's eyes. "Another treasure room!" she said. "Mad Jack must have hidden all his loot behind it!"

"I suspect there's a trap behind that door," Uncle Richard said. "Think for a minute. This is the only door we've seen in this whole mine. Even Mad Jack's chamber, with his crown in it, didn't have a door. What does that say to you?"

"It says to me that there's something even more valuable than a crown in there!" Al said. She turned to Stephen. "We can get it! Come on! Help me with this door!"

Uncle Richard stood still in front of the door. "I don't like this . . ."

Al shoved him out of the way. "The bandits will be back on top of us if we don't hurry." She tossed the crown to the floor and tested the doorknob. It turned in her hand.

"How about that? Not even locked!" She pushed against the door. It didn't budge. "It's a little stuck, that's all." She turned to Stephen. "Give me some help here. Just one good heave." The two of them pushed, but the door did not move an inch. Al grabbed the handle and rammed her shoulder into the door. "One good heeeee*oooooooo*!"

Stephen fell across the threshold, but there was no floor on the other side! Uncle Richard dragged him back from a gaping pit. The door swung wide over the emptiness, with Al clinging desperately to the knob.

"I could use a little help here," Uncle Richard said, seizing one of the iron bars on the door. "Grab hold around my middle." The two of them slowly hauled the big door closer to them. As soon as Al got in reach, they pulled her back onto solid ground.

She sat pale-faced, gulping for air. "Just one good heave!" Uncle Richard said. Al went from pale to red. Her eyes flashed as Uncle Richard bent to pick up the crown she'd dropped. "Very generous of you to leave this behind before your . . . er, flight." He handed it to her.

Al hefted the crown in her hand as if she wanted to hit him with it. Her breath hissed between her teeth.

She turned and kicked the wall. Then she went to the door and carefully closed it again.

"Why did you do that?" Stephen asked.

"I'm hoping that a bandit or two will go hurrying through it." Al turned and stalked away down the tunnel.

Stephen turned to Uncle Richard. He seemed to be interested in the stone wall next to the door. "Somebody's got to calm her down," he said. "And I guess I'm the only one for the job."

He started after Al, but she had gotten a pretty good lead. By the time he reached the end of the tunnel, Stephen still hadn't caught up with her. He crossed over into the large room, ducking his head under the low beam. Then a hand clamped over his mouth, yanking him upright. Stephen tried to break free, his shout muffled by the hand. He got one look at his captor's face, and his breath caught in his throat. The face was drawn and ghastly pale but very recognizable. It was Antonio Malvado.

13

ALONE IN THE DARK

SUNDAY; 1:21 P.M., *San Bernardo*

"Keep your mouth shut!" Antonio whispered, lifting a pickax into Stephen's view. "One word out of you . . ." Stephen's eyes were riveted to the sharp end of the pick as Antonio let go of his mouth.

Antonio snatched the mining helmet from Stephen's head and stomped on the lantern. The beam of light winked out. "Just a precaution—so you can't go off on your own."

In the faint light from Antonio's helmet Stephen could see how changed the man was. His once-immaculate white suit was crumpled and stained, and a large red blotch nearly covered the side of the jacket.

"No, I'm not dead," he said. "Le Vac and his

men rushed off before they could make sure of me. They were so busy chasing your uncle, they never bothered with me at all. So I was able to follow them. I came here"—he swayed slightly—"to punish them." His pickax came up. "To punish you all." Stephen realized that the eyes glittering under the miner's helmet were not quite sane.

"I am a dead man now. I'll never get out of these mountains. Le Vac must die too. So must your uncle. And you will help. . . ."

A clawlike hand closed on Stephen's arm, dragging him to the far end of the room. "I saw the woman enter a tunnel. But then you arrived—alone. And your uncle will look a little harder for you."

He dragged Stephen down another tunnel to a point under some sagging wooden supports. "This is where he'll find you, trapped under a collapsed beam. That's one of the things this pick is for," he said, shaking the tool. "A helmet lamp on the floor will illuminate your position. And when he steps into the light to help you, I'll be behind him." He smiled horribly. "That's the second thing the pick is for."

Stephen realized he couldn't stay still any longer. If he let Antonio get him under that beam, it would be all over. But how to escape? His mind raced.

Antonio stood right behind him. Stephen slammed his elbow back, right into the red stain. Antonio hissed. His grip slackened, but the pick swept down. Stephen dodged. The pick slammed into a rock with a clang.

Stephen ran into the darkness, trying to keep out of the beam from Antonio's helmet. But that was the only light in the room. Stephen blundered about, crashing into pillars, reeling around. He heard Antonio staggering behind him.

Zigzagging back and forth, Stephen smacked into a low beam. Another tunnel mouth! He crouched in the tunnel, looking out into the room. Antonio's helmet lamp swept around, occasionally getting cut off by one of the support posts. "I'll find you, boy," his quiet voice whispered across the room. "And when I do, you're dead."

Stephen didn't wait to hear any more. He set off down the tunnel, checking over his shoulder for that telltale helmet light. Finding his way wasn't easy. He did it partly by touch but mainly by bumping into things. I need a light, he thought. And I should be far enough away by now . . .

His fingers went to the buttons on the outside of his watch. Fumbling in the dark, he hit the wrong button. Letters began flowing across the dial. But with that little bit of light, Stephen saw the control he wanted. He hit it, and a thin, intense beam of light sliced out of the watch dial. Stephen swept the tunnel before him and moved forward. He brought his wrist in toward his chest, trying to hide as much of the glow as he could with his body. It wouldn't do for

Antonio to see light at the end of this tunnel, he thought.

Stephen moved quickly down the tunnel. Antonio could come wandering along at any moment. Just the thought had Stephen looking nervously over his shoulder. His breathing seemed unnaturally loud to his ears.

Of course, when Uncle Richard caught up with Al they'd realize something had happened. Then they'd start searching for him. They could eliminate the tunnels they were in. That left five others . . . where they stood an equally good chance of meeting Antonio and his pickax. Stephen went cold at the possibilities.

Visions of Uncle Richard and Al lying dead somewhere, Antonio tracking him down, Le Vac tracking him down, all went through Stephen's mind. The darkness seemed to press inward against the beam from his watch dial. It appeared to be dimming. How good is the battery on this thing supposed to be? he wondered. What if it dies on me? He bit his lips.

Then his heart leaped up. A big patch of light was moving up ahead! Stephen almost called out, then clamped his mouth shut. That patch of light was *too* big. He doused his watch light. And as the patch of light grew stronger, he was glad he had.

The beams of dozens of miner's lamps came questing at him like giant fingers. Stephen fell back a little to stay in the darkness. The bandits came marching on.

Stephen kept retreating until an unpleasant realization hit him. The bandits were herding him back to the large room—and for all he knew, into the arms of Antonio.

14

HIDE AND SEEK

SUNDAY; 1:33 P.M., *San Bernardo*

Stephen sped on silently, but now his eyes were desperately scanning the walls for a hiding place. A side tunnel, a pocket, fallen rocks, anything, he thought. Then in the half light from the helmets behind him, he saw a crevice. He squeezed into it just as the bandits came up.

There was no order in the way they straggled along. Stephen tried to push deeper into the crevice, only to discover that the lights had tricked him. His hiding place wasn't as deep as it looked. All he could do was freeze.

As more bandits came up, their lights made the area brighter and brighter. Stephen realized his hiding place was no such thing. All he needed was for one bandit to glance in his direction. . . .

A big knot of bandits came by. In the middle was Paul Le Vac. The bandit chief walked bent over, his arms crossed over his belly. With every step he cursed Uncle Richard. Stephen held his breath.

The bandits passed like some sort of nightmare parade, their lights glinting off rifle barrels and machete blades, off gold teeth and sweaty bodies. If he had wanted to, Stephen could have reached out and touched them. Certainly he could smell them. But all he could do was stand crouched in a cramped position and hope no eye fell on him. Miraculously none did, even though one of the bandits almost brushed up against him.

At last they had all passed. Stephen slumped out of his hole, then snapped back into it as a clump of stragglers came by. He didn't move even after they had all had gone. Drained, he peered after the receding glow of light.

I'll let them clear the way for me, he decided. Maybe they'll scare Antonio off. They're certainly looking for Uncle Richard and Al.

Stealthily Stephen began following the bandits through the tunnel. He stayed well back, far enough so that he could see the lights but not be caught in the lights himself. At every shadow he stopped and carefully checked things out, just in case Antonio had the same idea about hiding.

While he was looking behind a convenient pile of rocks he realized that the lights had suddenly stopped. Stephen peeked around a support beam to see why.

Le Vac stood with his men in the big room. "We

don't have enough men to search all these tunnels,"
he said. "I want one man to stay behind here; it
would be a good place for an ambush."

One of the men stepped forward, a brawny man
with no shirt and dirty hair. He took a long, sharp
blade out of his belt. "Anyone comes by, I'll slice
'em, then see who it is."

Le Vac nodded. "Fine, Raymond, if it's Duffy or
the brat. But if Señorita Sotelo is still with them, try
not to mark her up."

The hatred in his voice made Stephen's hair stand
up. "I never thought she would cross me." The scar
wriggled on his face like a white worm as he laughed.

Standing in the tunnel, Stephen felt a worse chill
than he had before. Could Al be in cahoots with him?
She could have told them we'd be on her plane.
What would have happened if she hadn't gotten hit?
Wild thoughts tumbled through his mind. But she
helped us, got us through all those traps right till we
found the crown. His eyes narrowed. Unless she
wants the crown for herself. Is that what Le Vac
means about her crossing him?

The bandits marched off. Raymond watched them
go down the tunnel, then stood alone in the large
dark room. He looked about nervously, his helmet
light cutting through the darkness.

Stephen crept out into the room, his eyes darting to
possible hiding places. If I position myself right, I'll
be able to see anyone coming down the tunnels. He
brushed against a support post. The old wood groaned.

"Who's there?" The bandit's light shot in Stephen's

direction. He froze behind the post. Raymond was moving his way, and Stephen couldn't retreat. Light from the lamp washed all around his hiding place. If Stephen moved, he'd be seen for sure.

Stephen held his breath. His whole world was a beam of light and the reflections off a long knife. But Raymond stopped and turned around. Stephen saw a shadowy figure dodge a knife thrust and sweep a leg into the back of Raymond's knees. The bandit abruptly knelt. He tried to claw his way up again, but the figure dug its hands into his throat. Raymond's arms moved wildly for a moment, then he collapsed like an empty sack.

The figure stepped into the light beam. "Stephen?" It was Uncle Richard.

Stephen broke into a grin of relief until he noticed Al there too. His face hardened.

"My gosh, kid, what happened to you—" she began, but Stephen cut her off.

"The bandits came through here." He pointed to the tunnel they'd taken. "And Antonio is—"

That's as far as Stephen got when a pickax came flashing down. Uncle Richard sidestepped, and the blow landed in one of the support posts. A hail of rubble came down, and Antonio burst into loud cursing. "You!" Uncle Richard said.

The echoing noise brought the bandits back down the tunnels. "Can't fight him *and* them," Uncle Richard said as the sounds of the mob came closer. He led them to another tunnel, running along at full speed, not even bothering about traps. Antonio recovered his balance and staggered along after them. The tunnel sloped upward steeply. He weaved back and forth as he made his way up, shaking the pickax.

They had traveled about thirty feet along the tunnel when they came upon a big metal box on wheels, blocking their path. "Some kind of ore cart," Uncle Richard said, squeezing by. "They must have used it to move the gold out. This must have been the entrance tunnel!" But beyond the cart stood a pile of ancient rubble. "Rockfall—cut off the old tunnel . . ."

Behind them Antonio had reached the ore cart. "We're trapped!" Al gasped.

Behind Antonio the bandits came boiling up the tunnel. Helmet lights caught Antonio as he was climbing up on the ore cart. He whirled, and was recognized.

A moan of superstitious terror rose from the bandits. The ones in the front ranks fought their way back until the whole group was bunched in the tunnel mouth. Antonio was quick to use their fears. "Punishment! I've come back to take you all!" He shouted horrible things after them. A few of the bandits turned and let off a few shots. The noise brought rubble down from the ceiling.

"Stop, you fools!" Le Vac's voice rose above the confusion.

Antonio had made it to the ground on the far side of the ore cart, safe from their bullets. Wild laughter came from him as he heard Le Vac. "Punish! Punish!" he yelled, shoving maniacally at the back of the ore cart. With a rusty groan it started moving down the incline.

The cart picked up speed, its rusty axles screaming. Antonio jumped on the back of the cart, still laughing. Faster and faster it rolled down the tunnel.

The bandits saw the cart zooming down on them, and scattered from the tunnel mouth. Uncle Richard started running after the cart to take advantage of the confusion, and the others followed.

But just before the cart came out of the tunnel, a wheel went flying off. The cart suddenly veered to the left. The bandits dodged away, but the cart plowed on into one of the old support pillars.

The ancient wood cracked; the ceiling groaned. "Get back . . ." The rest of Uncle Richard's words were lost as the ceiling fell in with a roar.

15

NO DEAL!

SUNDAY; 2:49 P.M., *San Bernardo*

Stephen, Al, and Uncle Richard crouched beside a support as the roar of falling rock filled their world. The beam quivered but held up. Stephen coughed in the rock dust, looking at the plug of rubble that filled the tunnel mouth. "That is definitely the end of Antonio," Uncle Richard said. "The rockfall came down right over the ore cart."

"Looks like it also came down on the bandits," Al said. "We won't have to worry about them."

Stephen looked around. "That just leaves worrying about how we get out of here. Both ends of the tunnel are blocked."

"Maybe not. I think Antonio did us a favor." Stephen followed his uncle's eyes to the hole that used to be a ceiling. What was that up there? Caves?

No! Tunnels—bigger than the ones they'd been scrambling through! This wasn't just a way out, it was a way back into the new mine!

Uncle Richard led them onto the shifting pile of rubble. It wasn't an easy climb. The stones beneath them kept moving, as if the pile were trying to swallow them alive. Being the lightest, Stephen pulled into the lead. But Al and Uncle Richard were right behind him when he worked his way onto the new tunnel floor.

They sighed in relief, then froze. Echoing shouts came from the distance. "Sounds like the bandits survived, and found their own route out," Uncle Richard said. "They're headed this way."

The three of them ran up slanting tunnels, away from the noise. "One good thing about this," Al said. "No booby traps!"

Yeah, Stephen thought, we have other things to worry about—like traitors.

Uncle Richard skidded to a halt in an intersection to check some numbers painted on the walls. "I know where we are now," he said. "Come on."

"Does this lead us back to the entrance?" Stephen asked.

"Not exactly," Uncle Richard said.

They ran through tunnels, came to intersections, and made sharp turns. Stephen lost all sense of where he was. His head was spinning; it hurt when he breathed. He could hardly lift his feet.

"How long have we been in this blasted mine?" Al panted out the words.

"Nearly nine hours," Uncle Richard said, looking at his watch. "We came in a bit after dawn, say, six o'clock. Now it's almost three P.M."

"Wonderful," Al said. "Have we done enough dodging to stop and rest for a minute?"

Stephen fell to the ground and gulped air through his mouth. Then Uncle Richard handed him a can of corned beef hash. He gulped it down.

"Duffy! Duffy!" Stephen nearly choked on the last spoonful of hash when the voice came down the tunnel. It was Paul Le Vac. "Look, I know you're there. Answer me."

They sat in silence.

"This time I've got you," Le Vac said, gloating. "No tricks will get you out. I want Jenson's crown."

"Not a chance!" Uncle Richard shouted back.

"My men are very angry with you," Le Vac shouted.

Al whispered, "I bet *he's* not too thrilled either."

Le Vac went on. "When they get you, they'll make you suffer before you die." Le Vac tried to make his voice sound reasonable. "But if you give *me* the crown, I'll make sure you leave this mine unhurt. My word of honor."

"Your word of honor?" Uncle Richard laughed. "Look, turkey, peddle that somewhere else. You're a murderous coward with no honor at all."

"Calling me names won't help. To get out of this mine, you've got to get through me and my men. We'll get the crown—clean or bloody!"

Le Vac ranted on, making wild threats and promises. Uncle Richard let him shout but motioned Stephen and Al to silence. He leaned toward the tunnel, listening intently to something besides Le Vac's voice. Stephen strained his ears, and finally heard what Uncle Richard had caught. It was a barely audible sound—bare feet shuffling on a rocky floor. Someone was creeping down the tunnel toward them.

Uncle Richard stepped behind a pile of rocks leaning against the wall. He took off his mining helmet, stuck it on top of the pile and remained behind the rocks in the darkness, waiting. Le Vac wound down his yelling. "This is it. Last chance, Duffy. Do I get that crown?"

"No deal!" Uncle Richard shouted.

"Take him, George!" A man darted from the tunnel. He leaped at the beam from Uncle Richard's helmet, a knife gleaming in his hand. George plunged the knife under the helmet and crashed into the rocks. Uncle Richard jumped on him. Judging from the noises that came out of the darkness, the rocks had been gentler to George.

"George? George?" Le Vac kept calling as shrieks came down the tunnel.

Uncle Richard's arm popped out of the darkness to scoop up his helmet. "This way," he said to Stephen and Al.

"Keep up with them!" Le Vac shouted from behind. "Don't let them get around us!"

"Le Vac and his merry men are still blocking us from the mine entrance," Uncle Richard whispered as he ran. "But there's another way out"—he panted—"if we can reach the mountaintop."

The tunnel led up to a large gallery. Rushing along, they nearly crashed into a wire fence. "An elevator!" Stephen said. "We can ride up!"

Uncle Richard worked the controls. " 'Fraid not," he said. "The generator is at the top of the shaft." He looked up into the darkness. "Must have been shut off when everybody left the mine." He pointed to a metal staircase that spiraled around the elevator cage-work. "We'll have to use this instead."

The metal rang with their footsteps. "What a goshawful racket," Stephen said. "The bandits won't have to guess where we went."

As they wound their way up the stairs, the metal began to ring with new footsteps, dozens of them, below them. The lamps on the bandits' helmets made a glowing blob that came spiraling up.

Stephen speeded up, but his strength began to flag. He tried counting steps, but by the time he got to 153, he was staggering. Keep yourself going up, he thought, and your lunch staying down.

"Just a little farther," Uncle Richard said.

They reached the end of the stairs and reeled dizzily for a moment. Then Al and Stephen collapsed on the landing.

"No time to rest now," Uncle Richard said, rushing them into a large stone room. "We still have to slow down those blasted bandits."

The place was filled with huge pieces of machinery. Stephen and Al gawked, amazed.

Uncle Richard stood beside a control panel. "I've got to start the generator," he said, manhandling a big drum of oil. "But first I need this to fix those guys downstairs."

Al and Stephen helped him push the drum to the top of the stairs. "Are we going to push this down on them?" she asked.

Uncle Richard handed her a hammer and chisel. "Just whack a few holes in it and let the oil drip down the stairs."

Al got down to business, making lots of holes for the oil to gurgle out from. She and Stephen maneuvered the barrel so that the oil flowed down the whole stairway. It soon reached the bandits, whom they could hear slipping and swearing below them.

Meanwhile, Uncle Richard sweated over the big generator. It took long minutes before the engine caught and turned over, but it finally roared into life, then started humming.

"Okay, Mr. Wizard, your generator is going," Al said. "But how will that get us out of here?"

Uncle Richard led Al and Stephen around the generator to a big hole in the wall. Stephen blinked in the first daylight he'd seen in hours. They stood on top of the mountain, and a pair of thick metal ropes stretched across a valley right to the top of the next mountain. The ropes were anchored into the rock over a big machine. And dangling from them was a metal box.

"A cable car!" Stephen said.

"It's how we move the gold ore. It goes up the

elevator and across the valley. That's as close as the railroad comes to us." Uncle Richard started working on the big machine.

"That's what we're going to escape in?" Al asked.

"You've got it." Uncle Richard smiled at the expression on her face.

Another piece of machinery suddenly whirred to life. But the smile left Uncle Richard's face as he saw a giant wheel begin to turn over the shaftway. "Very smart. They heard the generator going, so they ran down and started the elevator." He rushed back to work on the control box.

"Aren't you going to stop them?" Al asked.

"I can stop them, or I can get us out of here. There's only time for one," Uncle Richard answered, working frantically with the wires.

Stephen had the sinking feeling that time had run out. He glanced at his watch and groaned. Even if they got out of this spot, they'd never catch the seven o'clock plane back to New York.

The big wheel on top of the elevator reeled in more and more cable. The shouts of the bandits floated up the shaft.

"Hurry! Hurry!" Al cried.

"Keep your shirt on. Got to fix this so they won't control the cable car," Uncle Richard said. He reached into the control box. The cable car machinery behind him went into motion. Al climbed into the car, and Stephen scrambled in after her. I'm not leaving her alone with the crown, he thought.

The cable car started to move. "Uncle Richard!"

Stephen yelled. His uncle turned from the controls and ran for the car. Behind him the top of the elevator appeared in the shaft.

Uncle Richard's legs pumped as he ran for the moving car.

The side of the elevator cage came level with the floor. A bandit leaped out and sped after Uncle Richard. Crying "A hundred bucks!" he made a flying tackle, and wrapped his hands around Uncle Richard's legs.

The tackle brought Uncle Richard down, but even as he was falling he rolled himself into a ball, jerking his legs away from the tackler. They hit the ground together, but the tackler had lost his hold. Uncle Richard rolled after the cable car.

By the time he got to his feet the car had already passed through the opening in the mountain. The gap widened to several feet as Uncle Richard kept running, the bandits pounding after him.

Uncle Richard didn't look back. All his attention was on the cable car as he ran right to the edge of the mountain. Without missing a stride, he dived off.

16

STOP THE TRAIN!

SUNDAY; 3:14 P.M., *San Bernardo*

Uncle Richard flew down and landed half inside the cable car. His feet dangled in the air as Al and Stephen pulled him in to safety. The bandits stopped short at the edge of the mountain. None of them wanted to try *that* jump.

Uncle Richard looked at his watch. When he got his breath back, he said, "Good-bye, bandits; hello, home! And we're right on schedule!"

"I'd like you to tell me something about this precious schedule of yours," Al said. "So far we've got the crown and we're out of the mine. But what happens when we get to that mountain across the way? We've got to get down, and get through the jungle. So how do you think you'll get up to New York tonight?"

Stephen joined in with a comment of his own. "I want to hear this too. The last plane for New York leaves in less than two hours."

Uncle Richard smiled. "We'll ride." He went to the front of the cable car. Stephen and Al followed.

"I think I mentioned that the mountain over there is the closest the railroad ever comes to us," he said. "And, according to my . . . er, schedule"—he raised his eyebrows at Al—"the good old three-twenty should be loading up there right now. Take a look at the top of the mountain."

As they drew closer to the mountaintop, Stephen could see it had been leveled off. A couple of shacks and a big wooden water tower stood beside a loading platform and a set of railroad tracks that wound their way around the mountain. Men stood shoveling coal onto the tender of an old-fashioned steam engine. Behind it stretched a line of wooden railroad cars. "That's the most beaten-up train I've ever seen," Stephen said. "And right now, the most beautiful one too."

Al snorted. "It looks to me like something they left out to rust."

"That's a pilot talking, for sure!" Uncle Richard said, laughing. "It might not look like much, but that old workhorse will get us to Puerto Escobar in half an hour. Once we get to town, we get an airplane and fly to Fortaleza. There we catch the evening flight back to New York . . . and get home before your parents, Steve."

"That's great!" Stephen said. "But aren't you

forgetting about the bandits? For all we know, they may be back in the cave, breaking the engines for this cable car.''

''I have thought about that. There's nothing much they can do to the engines, and I don't think they'd try something stupid like cutting the cables.''

''R-r-real stupid,'' Stephen said. ''Why wouldn't they cut the cables?''

''Right now Le Vac doesn't want anything to happen to us,'' said Uncle Richard.

Al broke in. ''Then he's been doing a great job of *pretending* he wants to hurt us.''

''Oh, he'd like to see us dead, all right,'' Uncle Richard answered. ''But he wants the crown first. That's why he won't cut the cables. He'd scatter the crown—and us too—all over this valley.''

''Nice thought,'' Stephen said.

''No, if he's going to do anything, I expect he'll try to stop the train.''

Uncle Richard was right—the bandits did nothing. As the cable car moved smoothly over the lush green valley, Stephen sat back to enjoy the ride.

''This thing is worth a lot of money,'' Al said, taking out the crown. Her eyes went to Stephen. ''What would you do with a lot of money?''

He turned away. ''That would depend on how I got it.'' Still feeling her gaze on his back, he shrugged. ''I dunno. Probably buy all the video cassettes in the world.''

Al laughed. ''Well, what would *you* do?'' Stephen asked.

"Start some schools, I think." She smiled at his astonished face. "Believe it or not, I came here after college to be a teacher. We have very little money for schools or teachers, especially in these hills. Many people can't read or write."

Her face turned bitter. "I even tried to set up my own school here. But the money ran out and that pig Le Vac scared the pupils off. He thinks he's the lord of the hills, or something."

"So that's how he knew you!" Stephen said.

"He recognized me?" Al sighed. "He'll never forgive me for not 'serving' him. There goes the school. I guess I'll always be a pilot." She stuffed the crown back into her knapsack. Stephen got up and went to the front of the car to look at the train. The train crew hadn't noticed the cable car yet. They were still loading coal.

Uncle Richard began fiddling with his watch. He didn't seem to like what he saw. Stephen peeked over his shoulder to watch the flickering numbers.

"No getting around it," Uncle Richard said. "This cable car is running slow." His lips tightened. "Pablo always kept the machinery running at top efficiency. I guess when Antonio got rid of him, he let the machinery go too."

"Running a little late isn't all that bad, is it?" Al said. "Won't the train still be there?"

"Of course. We'll catch the attention of the train crew long before we actually arrive. I'm sure they'll hold the train for us."

"Hey!" Stephen said. "Look there! It's another cable car, coming in the opposite direction."

"This is a two-car system," Uncle Richard said. "When one car comes down, the other car goes up."

"That means there's a car coming up for the bandits to ride down in after us," Stephen said.

Uncle Richard looked at him in surprise. "You have a point, Steve. I hadn't thought of it that way." Then he shrugged. "But there's nothing to worry about. By the time the bandits make it over there, we'll be long gone on the train."

The two cable cars came closer and closer to each other, until they passed. "That means we're halfway across," said Al. "How are we doing on time?"

"I estimate we're going to be one minute and thirteen seconds late," Uncle Richard said. Little worry lines appeared around his eyes. "How are they coming along on that train?"

The train crew had finished loading the coal. Now one trainman went to the water tower. He pulled on a big chain. An enormous pipe swung down from the front of the tower. Water poured out, filling the train's water tanks.

"Now all they have to do is get their steam pressure up, and they'll be leaving," Uncle Richard said.

"Let's not start worrying over nothing," Al said nervously. "Everyone knows that railroads are famous for being slow. I'll bet anything that they'll wind up starting behind schedule."

"It would be just our luck to have the trains run on time," Stephen muttered.

The cable car came closer to the mountaintop. Wisps of smoke puffed out of the locomotive's smokestack. Still no one had looked up and noticed them.

"Maybe we should try to get their attention," Al said. She took a deep breath, and bellowed, "*Oye! OYE!* HEY! *COMPADRES!* LOOK UP! *AQUÍ!* HERE!"

None of the trainmen seemed to hear her. "Come on! All of us now!" Al said.

They yelled and screamed until they were hoarse. Stephen felt as if his throat were going to split open. But they might have been whispering, for all the effect they had on the train crew.

"The guns! We'll shoot off the guns! That will have to get their attention!" Al pulled out her pistol.

Uncle Richard drew his gun too. Both of them fired a few rounds into the air. In the car the noise was deafening. But the men on the ground didn't hear anything.

"Maybe the wind is blowing the sound in the wrong direction," Stephen said. "That must be why they don't hear us." Clouds of steam puffed out around the locomotive wheels. They could clearly hear the steam hissing.

Al's hand was clenched around the handle of her pistol. "Maybe we should shoot at their precious train," she fumed. "I'm sure they'd notice that."

"Better not. With our luck we would hit the boiler and make the whole blasted train blow up," Uncle Richard said. "And since we want it in one piece to get us out of here, we'll have to come up with something else. . . ."

"You'd better think of it quickly," Stephen said. "I think the train is leaving!"

They could hear the huffing sounds of the steam engine turn to chugs. The engineer pulled on the whistle as the wheels on the train started to move.

"Of course!" Uncle Richard suddenly said. "Why didn't I think of it before?" He dug frantically through his knapsack. "The flare gun! We still have one flare left. When I shoot it in front of them, they'll have to notice that. They'll *have* to stop!"

He slipped the flare shell into the gun, snapped it together, and stood up. "Aim it just ahead of them . . ."

The train picked up speed as it pulled away from the platform. Uncle Richard stretched out his arm, tracking the train, moving the flare gun slightly ahead of it. He pulled the trigger. Nothing happened.

"What's the matter?" Al asked.

"Something wrong with this shell." Uncle Richard pulled the trigger again, then a third time. The gun went off with a thump. They blinked their eyes in the dazzle of the flare.

Al recovered first. "Where is it going? It's flying off behind the train!"

"I aimed that gun perfectly," Uncle Richard said. "That blasted shell . . ."

The flare whizzed wildly through the air. Then it exploded—far behind the locomotive. The train roared on.

"W-we can't stop it," Al stammered.

Stephen gripped the edge of the cable car to keep his hands from trembling. "We've had it!" he mumbled. "There's no way out this time!"

17

THE END OF THE LINE?

SUNDAY; 3:23 P.M., *San Bernardo*

Al, Stephen, and Uncle Richard leaped down from the cable-car landing. They were just in time to see the last cars of the train pull out of sight down the mountain. "Well, good-bye, train," Stephen said.

His eyes whipped up to the other mountain, where the empty cable car was landing. The bandits piled into it. Stephen could see the sunlight glinting off their guns and knives. "And hello, bandits."

Uncle Richard stood on the railroad tracks, kicking at the loading platform. He hadn't said anything since his plan came apart. Al stood staring at the bandits' cable car. "They're coming," she said. Her voice was strained.

Stephen went over to his uncle. His eyes were shut. "Think, think, think," Uncle Richard said, still kicking the platform. He heard the scuffle of Stephen's shoes on the ground and turned. A faint smile came to his face. "It was a pretty good adventure up to here, wasn't it? All except for the getaway. Well, I suppose we could jump off this mountain—"

He stopped talking. His eyes widened. "Yes! Jump off the mountain!" It was the same old Uncle Richard who shouted, "Al, Steve, let's get over to those supply shacks. We'll need every piece of rope we can find!"

Moments later they came staggering out of the shacks, coils of rope over their shoulders and in their arms. Uncle Richard led them right to the edge of a flat ledge.

"Is this some sort of fancy rope trick you're going to show us?" Al asked. "You're going to lasso a mountain and swing down?"

"Close, but no cigar," Uncle Richard said, pointing over the edge. "Look down."

Stephen saw a long stretch of rocky mountainside dotted here and there with plants. Then came a flat area with railroad tracks.

"The train will have to pass through that area soon. If we really move, we can get down there and flag the train down. We can still get away."

They sat down with the rope coils and worked like madmen, tying them together into one super-rope. Every once in a while Stephen strained his ears, listening for the train, or looked to see how much closer the bandits had come.

"I have a question," Al said. "What happens if the bandits get here before the train gets down there?"

"Don't even think about that," Uncle Richard answered.

Al remained quiet and tied knots.

At last the rope was ready. Uncle Richard found a boulder and wrapped one end around it. Al and Stephen let out the other end of the rope over the ledge. Al's eyes were locked on the advancing cable car full of bandits; Stephen's were on the tracks. "Come on, train, come on!" he said. "First, you're too fast, now you're too slow!"

The cable car had nearly reached the landing. There was no sign of the train below.

"I guess that's it," Al said. There was the faintest trace of a squeak in her voice.

Uncle Richard cleared his throat before he spoke. "I guess so."

Both of them drew their guns and began checking them. "There's some good cover behind that pile of railroad ties over there," Uncle Richard said. "This boulder will do fine for me."

Al started walking to the place Uncle Richard had pointed out. But halfway there she stopped. She turned, took off her backpack, and tossed it to Uncle Richard. *"Por el niño,"* she said.

"What was that all about?" Stephen asked.

"You," Uncle Richard answered. "She said the pack was 'for the boy.' "

"What do you mean?" Stephen said. "What is Al giving me?"

Uncle Richard put out his hand. "Give me your knapsack, Steve." Stephen slipped off his pack. Uncle Richard opened it, then he opened Al's.

He took out the crown. The sunlight made the jewels sparkle, but it also showed how poorly the crown had been put together.

"Pretty ugly for something so valuable," Uncle Richard said. "Still, it led us into quite an adventure, didn't it, Steve?" He put it into Stephen's pack, then did up all the catches.

Stephen put the pack on his back. He turned to Uncle Richard. "Wait a minute—"

"No time to wait," Uncle Richard said. "The bandits are at the landing. You've got to be down the mountain before they get here."

Stephen opened his mouth to argue, but Uncle Richard cut him off. "Look, you don't want Le Vac to get the crown after all this, do you?" He pointed at the rope. "Get going."

"What about you and Al?"

"We'll get out of this somehow." Uncle Richard grinned. "That's been my business for years—getting out of scrapes."

"But . . ."

"No buts. I promised your mother I'd take care of you. So don't go making a liar out of me. Move it, Steve. I mean it."

Stephen said nothing as he took the rope and dropped over the edge. A quick good-bye wave, and the last thing Stephen saw was his uncle checking his gun.

Stephen made good speed down the mountainside,

going down the rope hand over hand. He even felt surefooted as his toes found places on the rock. But as he moved, something kept digging into his shoulder. Stephen looked to see what it was, and stopped dead. It was the last thing he expected to see—Uncle Richard's watch hooked on a strap of his knapsack. That means he's really in trouble, Stephen thought. Otherwise, he'd never let it go.

Tears stung his eyes when he saw there was a message on the dial. *Get home safe*, it said.

He can be as bad as Mom and Dad, Stephen thought, snapping off the message. Shunting me off like that with a "Get home safe." No way! We're partners in this!

Stephen began pulling his way back up the rope. He didn't know what he would do up there. He just knew that that's where he had to be.

He peeked over the edge of the ledge. Al and Uncle Richard were crouching behind some rocks. Paul Le Vac and the bandits stood on the railroad tracks. Are those all the guys he has left? Stephen wondered. Hardly a dozen men stood behind Le Vac. Maybe that track and field day down in the mine got a lot of them lost. Or maybe that's all he could fit into the cable car.

What the bandits lacked in numbers, they made up in meanness. Every one of them had a rifle or a machete in his hand. They marched in a group down the tracks. When they reached the water tower, Le Vac raised his hand. The bandits stopped. "Duffy!" he yelled.

Uncle Richard knelt in silence behind his boulder.

"You know, Duffy, you've annoyed me more in two days than most people do in a lifetime. I'm really going to enjoy this." Le Vac turned to his men. *"All right! Let's give it to them!"*

Stephen's gaze shifted from the bandits to something moving on the water tower. Not something, some*one*! But who? Uncle Richard and Al were still in their places.

The moment Le Vac gave his order, the mystery person jumped for the chain that controlled the flow of water. He grabbed it in midair and rode it down to the ground. With a groan the big pipe on the tower swung into position.

The bandits heard the noise. Le Vac looked up, open-mouthed. None of them knew what to expect.

What they got was water—hundreds of gallons of it, gushing out of a six-inch-wide pipe.

Stephen watched the torrent smash into Le Vac and knock him flat. He didn't get up. Half of the bandits were knocked out by the flood alone. The rest were thrown down by the water, losing their weapons. They lay on the ground, squirming, trying to keep from drowning in the instant flood.

Uncle Richard and Al ran toward the water tower, guns in hand. The mystery man stood by the chain, looking over the disaster and roaring with laughter.

He had the sun behind him, but Stephen could see that he wore a rumpled suit. And even in silhouette there was only one person in the world with ears as big—and as hairy—as that.

"Cutthroat Morton!" Stephen shouted in surprise. Uncle Richard heard him and skidded around.

"What do you think you're doing here?" His face hardened. "You're supposed to be down that mountain!"

Stephen grinned at him. "Yeah, but you forgot something." He held out the watch. "I had to bring it back."

Several expressions fought over Uncle Richard's face as he watched Stephen haul himself up. "What you did showed guts but no brains, Steve. Coming back into the arms of the bandits—" Uncle Richard gave him a look. "You risked your life! You didn't know how this would end."

"Well, what would you have done?" Stephen burst out.

Uncle Richard tried to keep a straight face but didn't succeed. "I'd have done exactly what you did, Steve. Just don't remind me! Now, let's move it!"

When they got to Cutthroat, he had shut off the flow of water. The soggy bandits were still lying dazed on the ground. "I think they've had the fight washed out of them," Cutthroat said.

Uncle Richard stared at him. "Cutthroat, how the—"

"I happened to be in the neighborhood, checking out trains for—uh—business reasons," Cutthroat said. "So I figured I'd stop by and see how you were handling things here." He looked down at the bandits. "Lucky thing I did too. Duffy, you got too much class to be done in by a buncha bums like these."

Little Wally, Cutthroat's partner, appeared from one of the supply shacks. In one hand he held a clump of short pieces of rope. In the other hand was a big knife. He walked down among the bandits, tying them up.

From the distance came a train whistle. "Oh, no! The train!" Al said. She dashed for the rope. "I'll stop it this time, even if I have to tie up the engineer!" She disappeared over the ledge.

18

BAD HABITS

SUNDAY; 3:53 P.M., *San Bernardo*

The train ride to Puerto Escobar was downright dull. Stephen sat back in his seat and closed his eyes as the train chugged its way out of the mountains. The bandits sat tied up under guard in a boxcar while Uncle Richard and company had a passenger car all to themselves.

Uncle Richard looked at his watch. "We'll reach Puerto Escobar in a few minutes, only three minutes behind schedule. Just a short flight from there—"

"If you don't see any suspicious types in jungle clearings," Al put in.

". . . and we'll arrive in Fortaleza . . . just in time for the flight back to the States. Perfect!"

The train slowed down as it reached the outskirts of town. Stephen roused himself from his doze and put out his hand to get his bag. But there was a hand already *in* his bag—Cutthroat Morton's hand.

Stephen blinked. "Hey, what are you doing, Mr. Cutth . . . er, Mr. Morton?"

Cutthroat jumped, then forced a smile. His hand came out of the pack with the gold crown in it. "Just wanted to see what started all the fuss," he said, leaning back.

Again Stephen noticed the cold eyes over the smile. This time it seemed the eyes were worse—even colder than before.

Uncle Richard shot to his feet. "Well, you had your look. Would you like to give it back now?" He held a hand out. The other hovered around his holster.

Cutthroat held the crown in the light. His other hand was hanging around the bulge in his suit. "It's a heck of a thing, gold an' jewels and all," he said.

"But hard as anything to fence," Uncle Richard pointed out. "Besides, you're getting all that reward money for the bandits."

Cutthroat glanced into Uncle Richard's eyes. "Yeah. Ain't that something!" He took one last regretful look at the crown. Then he glanced up and really smiled at Uncle Richard. His hand fell away from the gun in his suit, and he tossed the crown into Uncle Richard's hand. "Bad habits, Duffy. You know how it is."

The train had almost reached the station. "We're gonna get off here," Cutthroat said. "There may be some people we don't want to see waiting at the station. C'mon, Wally."

The little man popped up from behind Uncle Richard, pocketing his big knife. His face was red, as if he were embarrassed.

"Was he behind me all the time?" Uncle Richard asked.

"Yes, indeed," said Al, holstering her pistol. "But I was right behind him."

Opening the door, Cutthroat began to laugh. Wally jumped out. Cutthroat prepared to follow him.

"Good luck, Mr. Morton, wherever you go," Stephen called.

Cutthroat swung back. "You learn quick, kid." He winked, then he was gone.

"Ugh. I'm glad that's over," Al said. She stretched out her arms. "Now it's just back to Fortaleza and a normal life."

"Not quite," Uncle Richard said.

Suspicion crossed Al's face as she looked up. "What do you mean?"

Uncle Richard tossed the crown from hand to hand. "Somebody's got to register this treasure with the government," he said. "We can't do it. We have a plane to catch. Then there's the tax to be paid. And what will we do with the money that will come from this thing?"

Al's chin rose. "If you want my advice, I think a three-way split would be the fairest way to do it."

Uncle Richard frowned. "I think that's a little extreme."

Jumping to her feet, Al sputtered for a moment. Then a rush of words came out. "Okay, you just hired me as a pilot on this little adventure. But there was nothing in the contract about getting shot at, bitten at, and chased through a bunch of crazy traps. I thought you were a nice guy. Where do you come off, trying to cheat me out of a fair share?''

"I just don't think a third of the treasure is a fair share," Uncle Richard said. He raised his hand to cut Al off before she exploded. "I was thinking we should sign the whole treasure over to you. With Le Vac out of the way, that would help you get those schools you wanted off the ground. And buy a new plane while you're at it. What do you think, Steve?"

"Oh, I agree," Stephen said, saying good-bye to the mountain of videotapes he had been planning to buy with his share of the treasure. It's just my luck to have an uncle who thinks he's the Lone Ranger, he thought.

Al's mouth made a little O. She went pale, then bright pink. "I don't know what to say."

"Then say nothing. Start your schools. You can do something special for this country." Uncle Richard smiled. "I know what a special person you are."

Al's eyes sparkled over her pink cheeks. "I'll do my best," she said quietly. "You'll have to come and see . . . my schools . . . whenever you're in San Bernardo. For your mine, of course."

"Now *I* don't know what to say." Uncle Richard's eyes sparkled too.

Stephen turned away. "I know mushy stuff starting when I see it," he said.

Uncle Richard and Al laughed as they hugged each other. Stephen grinned and went to the other end of the car—to give them some time alone.

Later that afternoon Stephen and Uncle Richard sat in the airport at Fortaleza.

"Flight 555 to New York now boarding," the loudspeakers said. With a big smile on his face Uncle Richard got up and started walking. "Hey," Stephen said, "you forgot your bag."

"Did I? Well, well." Uncle Richard picked it up and walked along without another word, the big smile still plastered on his face.

Stephen tried to get him talking as they joined the crowd at the boarding gate. "Where do you think Cutthroat Morton went off to?"

"Who knows?" Uncle Richard said. That smile was beginning to get on Stephen's nerves. " 'Bad habits . . .' " Uncle Richard sighed. "I've got them too, being a loner all these years." The sappy smile smeared itself across his face again. "But a person can change, can't he, Steve? I mean, I'm not so old that I couldn't settle down, enjoy life, meet someone . . ."

"Humph," Stephen said. "I liked you better when you were always saying 'Move it!' "

19

TOOTHPASTE
AND PIPE SMOKE

SUNDAY; 9:47 P.M., *New York*

Stephen slept most of the way on the plane trip back
to New York. Even during the cab ride from the
airport he was still groggy. Uncle Richard sat quietly
beside him. As usual, the closer he got to home, the
more nervous he became. Suddenly he began talking.

"One of these days we're going to be just a little
late getting home. Your parents will be there, and
they'll want to know what in heaven we were doing.
I keep wondering what we'll ever tell them. Steve, I
know I can depend on you not to say anything . . .
rash. I mean, your mother would get very upset. . . ."
His eyes looked haunted.

Stephen shook his head. "I don't get it. You fight
alligators, but you're afraid of my mother!"

Uncle Richard looked out the window. The slow

traffic around them brought a worried look to his face. Stephen realized his uncle had been looking at his wrist for the whole cab ride, but there was no watch on it. Stephen had it.

He undid the strap of his knapsack. "You should have asked me for this earlier," Stephen said, handing the watch to Uncle Richard.

"I didn't want to disturb you." Uncle Richard slipped on the watch and hit some controls. He sat back with a jolt. "It's 9:53," he said. "Blasted traffic! Your parents are due home in another seven minutes."

That brought Stephen wide awake. "Ohmigosh!" he said. "What are we going to do?"

The taxi crawled along in traffic, crossing the bridge into Manhattan. A few minutes later it was rolling down his block. He looked ahead to his house and his heart almost stopped. A taxicab stood there, and its door was just opening.

Stephen groaned. "To come all this way and get caught over just seven minutes!"

"Four and a half minutes," Uncle Richard corrected him, looking at the watch. Their taxi pulled up right behind the other one. "I guess we'll just have to get out and face the music."

They both took deep breaths and opened the door. But the people stepping out of the other taxi weren't Mom and Dad. "It's the snooty Van Horns from across the street!" Stephen whispered. "Come on, Uncle Richard," he said. "We can still make it!"

They dashed up the stairs at Number 224½. "*Yay!*

It's still dark in there!'' he cried. Uncle Richard burst
through the door and turned on the lights, then hus-
tled Stephen into the dining room.

"First things first. Get out of those clothes. We
need to get rid of them right away!"

Stephen dumped his knapsack on the table and tore
at his dirty jungle clothes.

Uncle Richard bundled them up. "Next we get
cleaned up—fast!" They zoomed up the stairs.

Stephen's folks came in the door at 10:08, com-
plaining about the traffic from the airport. Uncle
Richard was downstairs to greet them, wearing fresh
clothing. Stephen smelled pipe smoke and grinned.
Uncle Richard had pulled out all the stops. He was
smoking the pipe Dad gave him for Christmas, and
even had the TV set on.

Stephen was brushing his teeth when his parents
and Uncle Richard came into the hall outside the
bathroom.

"He's up late for a school night," Mom said.

"Yes, he is, but he wanted to wait up for you so
much," Uncle Richard said. "We watched a little
television, then I sent him up here to get ready for
bed." He raised his voice a little. "How is it going
in there, Stephen?"

"I'm brushing my teeth."

Dad spoke in a low voice, but Stephen could hear
him. "I can't tell you how much we appreciate your
being around to keep an eye on Stephen. At his age
he really needs a firm influence around to keep him
out of trouble."

"I wish we could find someone else," Mom said. "It's not that I don't trust you, Richard. It's just that—I really don't know how to put this . . ."

"It's just that you don't trust me," Uncle Richard said. He sounded as if he yearned for nice, simple problems, like Paul Le Vac.

Stephen opened the door to rescue him. "Hi, Mom! Hi, Dad! How was the convention?"

Dad grinned. "They told me that two weeks of health food would get rid of this," he said, patting his stomach. "How about you? Have any adventures?"

Uncle Richard choked on his pipe smoke.

"It was a really neat weekend, Dad," Stephen said, his eyes twinkling. "Uncle Richard took great care of me!"

Out of the corner of his eye Stephen saw his mother looking suspiciously at Uncle Richard, who was loosening his shirt collar.

"By the way," Dad said, "I found this lying on the dining room table." He held out Stephen's knapsack. "Do you know what these are?" One of the quartz crystals from the mine lay in his hand.

Uncle Richard's mouth opened, but nothing came out.

"They're mine," Stephen said, his blue eyes sparkling. "For my rock collection. I found them while I was out with Uncle Richard." He took the pack and the crystal and headed for his room.

Behind him Dad said, "That boy! If he's not watching a movie, he's starting a new collection! You're a better man than I if you can keep up with him!'' He shook his head. So now it's rock hunting! Just once I wish he'd get interested in something practical.''

"I don't know about that, Jim," Uncle Richard said. "Stephen showed me some things about rocks this weekend that I'm sure I'll find very profitable.''

Stephen ran up the stairs, holding back a laugh.

RACE AGAINST TIME™

Join the race right at the start . . .
Become a RACE AGAINST TIME Adventurer NOW!

Your first top-secret assignment is to fill in the coupon below and join other fans of Stephen Lane and Uncle Richard in finding out more about the exciting world of RACE AGAINST TIME.

Yes, I would like to become a RACE AGAINST TIME adventurer.

Please send me FREE OF CHARGE:

(1) a RACE AGAINST TIME badge
(2) a membership card with my own personal code number
(3) a secret letter from Uncle Richard and Stephen

Name _____ Age _____

Address _____

_____

_____

I found out about RACE AGAINST TIME books

from _____

Send to:
RACE AGAINST TIME,
Armada Paperbacks,
8 Grafton Street,
London W1X 3LA.

Australia, *send to:*
RACE AGAINST TIME,
Armada Paperbacks,
Wm. Collins Pty Ltd.
P.O. Box 497,
Sydney, N.S.W. 2000.

✦✦✦✦✦✦✦✦✦✦
RACE AGAINST TIME

Adventure where *every second* counts!